# HER REVENGE

## JADE PRESLEY

## CONTENT WARNING

This book contains some depictions of emotional abuse, violence and gore, and sexual content with multiple consenting partners. I've taken every effort to handle these issues sensitively, but if any of these elements could be considered triggering to you, please take note.

*To all my marvel-loving, spice-reading queens and kings out there!*
*This is all for you!*

## ALSO BY JADE PRESLEY

Her Villains

Her Revenge

The Assassins (Coming summer 2022)

# CARI

"You can't honestly think we need to dispatch an entire unit," Chador, one of the males on the All Plane high council, says.

He's a handful of years older than me and wears the sun emblem of All Plane royalty on his maroon shirt. He waves his arm over the circular table the council and my four husbands gather around, a holographic map of the Shattered Isle poised over the flat surface.

"The Shattered Isle king made plans with our father to execute us and take control of fifty percent of the realms," Steel says, his muscled arms crossed over his chest.

I can feel the frustration flickering down our bond from where I sit in a cushioned chair a few feet away.

"Would you have us allow that behavior to go unchecked?" Steel continues. A muscle in his jaw ticks as he stares Chador down, and a lick of heat shoots across my skin. I would never want to be on the receiving end of Steel's anger—he's calm and kind and collected so much of the time, but when he's crossed? All bets are off.

"Of course not," Chador says, rolling his eyes. "I'm merely saying you don't need to steal twenty percent of our armed forces in order to check him."

"*Steal* them?" Tor snaps, lightning crackling in his eyes. The hair on the back of my neck stands on end from the electricity rippling off of him. "We're the kings of the All Plane," he continues, his voice rough. "Not to mention I've been their head commander for longer than you've sat on this council." Chador's eye twitches at that. "If I want to send our entire army to the Air Realm for no other reason than to host a six-week course on the proper way to sharpen a blade, then that's my right."

"Six whole weeks on blade sharpening?" Lock says, arching a dark brow at Tor. "Sounds horribly dull."

"Maybe you should go alone, Prince Lock," Chador says. "You're used to killing things. This should be an easy mission for you—"

"*King*," Lock says, his eyes sharp as he glares at Chador. He turns slightly, his long hunter-green coat shifting with the movement.

I hold my breath.

Hell, even Tor holds his breath as we watch.

"As a member of the esteemed high council of the All Plane, you should be able to remember titles. If you can't, perhaps your seat would be better served with someone else sitting on it."

Chador swallows hard, then shakes his head. "Our forces need to stay here more than ever," he says and throws a desperate look at the other five council members crowded around the table. He gets two begrudging nods and three outright looks of disapproval. "With the execution of our king—"

"Our father took up arms against us," Talon says, his voice ice-cold. "We had no choice. If you have doubts, I'll replay the footage my sleeper drones captured."

Chills burst over my skin, my blood crystalizing with frost. Talon's sleeper drones—tiny, almost imperceptible robots— were stationed all over the palace. They recorded everything, an order set forth by his father centuries ago. We'd seen the footage, and had to play it several times in order to prevent a rebellion from those who thought my husbands had murdered their father for the throne. The footage proved otherwise, but watching it...

Seeing their father wield his powers against his own sons, watching him admit to ordering hits on them...

Watching my own father escape my grasp...

Ice chills my hands, adrenaline coursing through my blood, demanding action.

Chador blows out a breath, bracing his knuckles on the table. "There is no debating the footage," he says through his teeth, pointing one finger at the holographic rendering of the Shattered Isle palace.

My *home*. Its magnificent structure sits on the centermost section of our great island. The midnight ocean I love so much stretches around it farther than I can see. Something sharp pricks my chest. A sense of longing that's immediately followed by a heavy dose of shame.

"But the All Plane has never taken war lightly," Chador continues. "You show up there with enough armed forces to take the island and you'll terrify the other realms into thinking they're next. They'll start prepping for war too. It'll be chaos."

Talon glances at Steel, and they hold some silent, contemplative conversation.

"You don't need the All Plane army," Chador says. "You need two good warriors. Everyone knows the Shattered Islers are soft of mind and weak of spirit, thanks to the stars and moon they worship." His nose turns up. "Take out the king once and for all, and then make plans to educate the people of the Isle on the correct way—"

The sound of my ice dagger cuts off his words as it sinks into the table an inch from where his hand rests.

Everyone turns their attention to me.

Lock smirks, his eyes glistening with mischief. "That was naughty, darling," he says, pride sizzling down our bond.

Chador's gulp is audible as I rise from my seat, strolling to the table. Talon and Lock immediately shift to make a place for me to stand. I focus on Chador. "It's that kind of talk that separated our two great realms for centuries," I say, tilting my head. "When was the last time you visited the Shattered Isle, Councilor Chador?"

He parts his lips, glancing at the other council members before returning his eyes to me.

"I'll take that as *never*," I say, and he presses his lips into a firm line. I nod. "Do us a favor and don't speak on subjects you know nothing about. *My* people are innocent of the crimes of my father." Most of them. Some—like Father's warriors and generals and devout followers—would face consequences, but that would be *after* we defeated my father. "And they are in no way 'soft of mind and weak of spirit.'" I roll my eyes. He didn't have a clue how amazing my people truly were. None of them did, honestly. And that's why we were here planning and strategizing to correct that wrong.

Tor grins at Chador, but there is nothing friendly about it.

"*Apologize,*" Lock says, shifting so he towers over Chador.

Chador grinds his teeth, glaring at the other council members, who remain silent. "Forgive me," he says.

Lock tilts his head, an eyebrow raised. "My queen," he says, drawing out the words like he's teaching a youngling to talk.

Chador looks like he'd rather be beheaded then address me by my new title. And while the idea is tempting, it's not what he deserves.

"It's fine, Lock," I say, drawing my husband's attention. The eyes of the council members follow. "It's been one day," I continue. "It will take time for your people *and* your advisors to adjust to our new situation."

Lock purses his lips, planting me with a look that sends heat spiraling right down the center of me. "Our new situation?" He strolls up to me, sliding one finger down the side of my neck. "The one where you're our mate, our wife, our queen? *That* situation?"

I try to keep the political mask in place, but it slips, just a fraction, as I bite back a smile.

5

"Yes," I say, slightly breathless from the way he's looking down at me, from how close he stands.

"I can only speak for myself," Maia, the lone female council member, says. "But change has been a long time coming." She dips her head to me, then my husbands. "I stand with you because I believe you will be the change the All Plane *and* the Shattered Isle needs."

I offer her a small smile and nod. In the future, when we are granted time not hindered by battles and threats, I want to get to know her better. She showed her character by challenging the All Plane king when he tried to convince them to pass a vote to execute his sons—my husbands—and for that alone, I'll be in her debt.

"Thank you, Maia," Talon says, then glances at the other members. "I am not my father. My brothers are not my father. You have a choice now, but *only* now. If you plan to fight or oppose us because of our new alliance, then speak now or simply leave. We will not take action against you." He eyes Chador, but the male doesn't budge an inch. "If you stay, then do so knowing that Cari is our wife and your queen and you will treat her as such. From this moment on, you are loyal to her and to us."

I hold my breath, my nerves tangling. Asking them to accept me isn't a new concept—they've been prepped since the weeks before our bonding ceremony—but declaring war for their new queen is another matter entirely.

The room is silent, not even a peep from Chador, who obviously isn't my biggest fan.

"Good," Talon says, waving an arm toward the grand double doors on the opposite side of the room. "You're dismissed. We'll inform you of our final plans tomorrow."

The council members slowly file out of the room, and I breathe a little easier once the doors shut behind them.

Steel reaches over the table, yanking out my dagger embedded into the wood. He spins it in his hand, then expertly throws it across the room, the tip sinking into a beam. He turns to me, an amused look on his face.

"I know," I say before he can get a word out. "I'll do better."

Steel furrows his brow. "What do you mean?"

I sigh. "I shouldn't have reacted that way," I say, eying the new hole in the table. "It will take your people time to adjust to me. And twice as long for the lies about *my* people to fade from their minds. I can't throw a fit every time someone insults them."

"Sure you can," Lock says.

"I like it when you throw daggers," Tor adds.

I bite back a smile, but it fades when I see the serious look on Talon's face.

"I *will* do better," I vow to him.

He blinks a few times, then shakes his head. "We all have to," he says, eying the map still on the table. He rubs his palms over his face. "I wasn't expecting to go to war so soon after taking the throne." He looks at me, a broken smile on his lips. "Some honeymoon."

"We're not going to war," I say, and each of my husbands turns a curious glance my way. I swallow hard and point to the spot on the map where my dagger hit. "Those coves conceal secret entryways into the palace," I explain. "We don't need an army. If we take out my father, then most of the Shatter Isle warriors will follow me, *us*."

"Does your father know about these tunnels?" Lock asks.

"He knows about these," I say, dragging my finger through the map and around the palace, down the beach, and pause on another set of coves. I glance up at Talon, who flinches at the sight.

The same place where The Great War started, where a young Talon saw my father murder his mother. I flash him an apologetic look and return focus to the spot I'd mentioned before.

"These tunnels," I say, tapping on the spot. "I made myself."

"How?" Tor asks.

"Ice and patience and a friend sworn to secrecy," I say, a ghost of a smile on my lips.

Gessi. My friend, my handmaiden blessed with the gift of earth manipulation. We worked for months creating the tunnels that aided in our adventures outside the palace. It was our escape route for when royal pressures mounted.

"All I have to do is make it to that cove, slip inside the palace, and slit his throat." A lump forms in my throat. "No war. No warriors' lives at risk. Just me."

"You're not going alone," Steel says.

"Of course, she's not going alone," Tor agrees.

"I was raised as an assassin," I counter. "I'll be fine—"

"You never have to do anything alone ever again," Lock says.

"You're needed here," I argue. "Your people need you more than ever right now. If their kings leave, it'll be like asking for open rebellion."

"She's not wrong," Talon says, then shakes his head. "But you're not going alone. We're coming with you," he says. "You have no idea what you might face. Once your father reaches the isle, he'll surround himself with all manner of protection—guards, warriors, contraptions fueled by his powers. He knows you'll come for his head and he won't make it easy."

I don't argue, because he's right. It will be a hard fight, one I'm not sure I'll survive, but I can't let him take out his anger on our people. Which he will. He didn't expect to lose his newly formed alliance with the All Plane king so quickly— and all the realms promised to him along with it. He'll be livid, and I know right where he'll place that wrath.

My home. My people. They are innocent and I won't allow them to pay for his mistakes.

"If you four go with me," I say. "Who ensures that someone like Chador won't try to usurp the throne?"

Talon glances to Tor, and they both grin at the same time.

Steel looks between the two brothers, then nods.

"Storm," Talon says.

"And River," Tor adds.

I glance at Lock, who merely nods before leaning down to whisper in my ear. "Talon and Tor's best friends and most trusted right hands."

"They'd die before letting anyone steal the throne from us," Talon says.

"And they'll keep the peace while we're away," Tor adds.

I raise my brows at Steel. "What about your best friend?" I ask.

Steel parts his lips—

"Blaize is a liability," Talon says before Steel can speak.

"You've never given him a chance," Steel argues.

"He betrayed our father—"

"Who just tried to kill us," Steel says, his hands fisting at his sides as he faces his brother.

Talon opens and shuts his mouth a few times. "Blaize is reckless. You know that. He's a wildcard, his values shift as easily as the wind."

Steel shakes his head. "He's a good male," he says. "He's never let me down before."

"And when we return, you can appoint him your personal guard for all I care, but I will not leave the fate of our realm in his hands." Talon's words are final, and he turns to Tor. "Let's hunt down Storm and River," he says. "I'm sure father sent them and their warriors off on a mission before we returned to ensure they weren't here to defend us." He sighs, then glances at me. "We'll see you for dinner?"

I nod, my heart twisting at the tension between him and Steel.

Tor winks at me before following Talon out of the room.

I reach for Steel, but he's already moving across the room. "I need air," he grumbles, then disappears through the doors, the sound of them slamming behind him echoing through the room.

Lock whistles. "That never gets old," he says, a playful smile on his lips.

"They do that a lot?"

Lock nods. "One of the few things Talon and Steel ever fight about is Blaize." He shakes his head. "Steel rarely has blind spots, but Blaize is one of them."

"Is he truly a rogue like Talon says?"

Lock shrugs. "As much as I am, I suppose." His grin turns animalistic as he shifts closer, his hands grazing down to my hips.

I arch into his touch, gasping slightly as he draws me against his body. "We'll have plenty of time to talk about them later," he says. "Right now, there are more important things to discuss."

Flames slide over my skin as he moves me closer to the council table, lifting me so I sit on the edge. "Such as?" I ask, my heart beating wildly in my chest.

I know we *should* be preparing for our journey and for the battle we're about to face, but if I can steal a few blissful moments with him, I will.

He spreads my thighs, the silk of my dress climbing up my legs with the motion, and he steps between them. "Such as," he says, tangling one hand in my hair, the other disappearing beneath the hem of my dress. "How hard you want me to fuck you on this table."

A warm shiver dances over my body and everything inside me narrows to the feel of his fingers teasing the lace covering my heat. The featherlight touches awaken every nerve ending in my body, and I smile up at him.

"Do your worst," I challenge, and his blue-green eyes churn.

He leans down, so close our lips almost touch, and he holds me there in delightful anticipation. Tendrils of shadow curl from his shoulders, snaking down his arms until they lovingly coil around my wrists—

I'm tugged backward, my spine kissing the council table as his shadows secure my arms over my head, two more soft-as-silk wisps twining around my ankles and spreading my legs apart.

My breath is ragged as I look at Lock.

Slowly, he peels off his jacket and tosses it on the other side of the table.

Meticulously, he rolls up the sleeves of his sleek black shirt.

"You really shouldn't have said that," he says, his grin predatory as he raises his hands, shadows dripping from his fingers and curling their way over my body, teasing and torturing me with silky caresses. "Let's begin."

## 2
## LOCK

*I* stalk around the council table, my eyes trailing over Cari's sumptuous curves, her smooth cobalt skin, her dark hair, and eyes that are screaming *fuck me*.

*All in good time*, I silently send the words into her mind.

She mentally opens for me in a way no one ever has, in the way only a bonded mate can, and my knees nearly buckle from the sensation. Her mind is full of obsidian coves like those of her beloved Isle, and each one is currently tinted with the fiery hue of lust.

For *me*.

Her desire swirls in my mind, begging me to touch her, taste her, take her.

My shadows hold her in place even as she tugs against her restraints, trying to reach for me as I walk in circles around her.

"This table has held many meetings," I say, my voice a whisper between the two of us in the massive council room.

"Carved from the mythical floating trees that populate our orchards, it's served as a constant centerpiece for all political matters of the All Plane realm for generations."

Cari arches her neck, looking at me upside down as I stop behind her. I brace my fists on either side of her head, caging her in without touching her.

"Wars were started at this table. This is where my own father declared me a fugitive and gave his warriors license to capture and kill me."

Cari trembles, and I lean forward to hover my face an inch above hers, so close my forehead nearly touches her chin.

"I'll end them," she whispers, lifting her head to brush her lips against mine. "I'll end anyone who attempts to carry out those orders."

I move just out of her reach, smirking down at her, relishing the lick of possessiveness flaring down our bond. Our mate has claws, and I fucking love it.

"I would watch you slaughter your way through an entire realm," I say, tightening the shadows around her wrists and ankles another fraction.

A pleasure-laced whimper escapes her throat, the sound sending licks of flame through my blood. My cock hardens, begging to sink inside her sweet pussy and make her scream my name.

I lean over her again, giving her a delighted grin when she remains still. She's quick to figure out my little game. "All the history surrounding this table, all the power that has sat around it—none of it compares to what you do to me, Cari," I say, the words gliding off my tongue with nothing but truth for once.

14

I delight in the games between lies, but with my mate? There is no need. She sees every dark piece of my soul and doesn't cower, doesn't try to shape me into something I'll never be.

"And now I'm going to fuck you on it until the memories of this council table's past are erased and replaced with nothing but the future you're bringing to our kingdom."

"Promises, promises," Cari teases, her eyes lingering on my lips that hover an inch above hers.

"Impatient little thing, aren't you?"

"When it comes to you?" she asks, biting on her lower lip. "Always."

My resolve shakes with her declaration, the sensation so fucking freeing after having so many people never see me for who I truly am. To be desired for *me* and not my title or the thrill of dancing with a monster.

I lower my lips to hers, grazing her mouth with a quick kiss before I draw back.

Cari growls, the frustration clear in the way she shifts her body in the only way her restraints allow.

I stalk around the table, trailing my fingers along its curves as I do, a breath away from touching her. She tracks my movements with a hunter's gaze that has my dick hardening to the point of aching.

"You told me to do my worst, darling," I say, bracing myself at her feet. "Don't you know who you're dealing with? Haven't I shown you by now?" I grin down at her, towering over her as she's helplessly secured to the table. Memories of our first time together when I was locked in that damned cell flare to life behind my eyes. "I can keep you here for hours," I continue. "I can bring you to the edge and push you away a thousand times and only when you're begging me, *moaning* at me to put you out of your misery will I comply."

Panic and curiosity flare in her eyes, the same emotions quivering down the bond so heavily I almost laugh. She must know I don't have that kind of willpower when it comes to her, right? It would take me centuries of practice to get to the point where I could keep from touching her for that length of time, but it's a fun image to paint all the same.

I wet my lips, tilting my head as I examine her. "Where shall I begin?"

I flick my wrist and another shadow spirals toward her, the edges of it caressing her breast. "Here?" I ask. "Or perhaps here?" Another flick, another shadow, this one gliding over her stomach. I guide the two shadows over her body in featherlight touches, and she arches against them, her body begging for more.

"Anywhere," she says, slightly breathless. "Everywhere."

"No, that won't do at all," I tease. "I know where you *really* want it." I spear my power into my shadows, combining the two teasing tendrils into one thicker stream, and gently guide it up her calf and between her thighs—

"Lock!" Cari gasps as my shadow slides and coils and caresses her pussy, one tendril stroking inside of her at the same time another breaks off to tease her clit.

"Yes, darling?" I say, feigning calm when truly my heart is racing as I watch her arch into her pleasure. I can feel the heat of her flickering across my power, can scent her arousal like the sweetest perfume.

"You...I...night *damn* me," she all but moans as I continue to work her with my shadows. I can feel her rock against them, can sense her body tensing as I swirl the cool wisps around her heat, giving her all the pressure she needs only to lighten them to barely-there touches. "Lock," she begs. *"Please."*

She tugs against her restraints, her forehead puckered with need, the power inside her rising up and begging to be released. If I'm not careful, my mate will turn me into a living ice sculpture.

"I haven't even touched you yet, darling," I say, slowly unclasping my belt and sliding it through the loops. I let it fall to the floor, all the while torturing her with my power. She's so lost in the sensation, she doesn't see me shed my pants, doesn't see me bare before her.

And it's glorious to watch. Her losing herself to what I'm doing to her.

"That feels amazing," she says, her eyes closed, back arched, thighs pressing together as if she needs the extra relief.

Well, that won't do at all. Not for the game we're playing.

I glide another shadow toward her, wrapping the two ends of it around her knees and pulling until she's spread wide before me.

She gasps, her eyes snapping open and locking on mine.

I give her a devious smirk and shudder when she drinks me in. Her eyes trail along every inch of my body, hazy and needy.

*"This* feels amazing?" I ask for clarification, fluttering the shadows teasing her clit.

"Yes," she breathes.

I spin the shadow, spiraling it against her clit over and over again until her entire body starts to shake.

"Night damn me," she says. "*Yes.*"

She clenches tight around the shadow I pump inside her, her hips thrusting upward as I continue to wind her up, to drive her toward that edge she's desperate to fall over.

"You're stunning," I say, gripping the edges of the table so hard I hear the wood groan. Sun and stars, I want to sink into her, but this is too much fun. Watching her writhe beneath my power, watching her yank at those restraints but unable to break them. "You're completely at my mercy, darling," I say, my eyes zeroing in on where my shadows slide in and out of her. "You realize that, don't you?"

She releases a shaky breath, then looks at me. "Yes."

I wet my lips, slowing my shadows enough that she whimpers. "And that doesn't scare you?" I ask, even though I know it doesn't. She's unflinchingly brave, sometimes to a fault, but I just love to hear her say it.

"No," she says, defiant. "Like I said before, do your worst."

A low growl rumbles in my chest, and I use my shadows to force her knees apart another inch.

"You are a brave little thing, aren't you?" I say, stroking her until she's writhing again. "Are you going to soak my shadows, mate? Is that what you want? What you need?"

"Yes," she says, practically keening the word as she arches off the table.

I drink it in, watching her, feeling her need spiraling along our bond. I grind my teeth to stop from groaning at the sight, at the sensation. Sun save me, this female is every dream and fantasy and danger rolled into one.

"You're going to come for me now, darling," I demand, sliding the cools wisps of shadow in and out of her while swirling the other over her clit.

Her back bows off the table, her arms and feet restrained, her knees spread apart as she moans, her entire body shaking as she shatters for me. Fuck, she's gorgeous. All breathy sighs and whimpers as I work her through the throes of her orgasm. And only when she relaxes, only when she opens those hazy eyes to look at me, do I draw all my shadows back.

"Good girl," I say, then wrap my hands around her ankles and yank her to the edge of the table where I stand, settling my hips between her thighs.

She moves to sit up, but I gently push her back down. "I like you splayed on this table," I say, and she grins up at me and locks her legs around my back, urging me closer.

"And I like you inside me. Now," she demands.

Heat licks up my spine, and I grin down at her. "Needy mate."

"Always," she says, then trembles when I line my hard cock up with her pussy, slick from what I just did to her.

I slide in an inch.

Then another.

So slow the breath in my lungs hitches as I savor her. She's searing heat and soft silk and she feels so fucking good around my dick.

19

Her thighs clench around me once I'm seated to the hilt, but I hold us there, simmering in that exquisite anticipation. I palm her ass in one hand, then run my other down the center of her chest, trailing my fingers over her clit then back up her stomach, over her breasts, teasing her nipples before tracing the column of her throat. She reacts to every touch, her body so fucking responsive it takes every ounce of strength I have to hold still, to keep stretching her pleasure out until she snaps.

Her pussy flutters around my cock, and I groan as she lifts her hips up, seating me deeper inside her. And when I don't tell her to stop, she does it again.

The leash I held myself on snaps with her trying to take the reins.

I grab her ass with both hands, hefting it off the table while she's still on her back, and I slam into her.

"Lock," she groans, trembling as I pull all the way out only to thrust inside again.

I pump inside her, furious and hungry, lava rushing through my veins each time I hit that sweet spot deep inside her.

"Fuck," I growl. "You feel so damn good." I stress every word with another thrust, so hard her breasts are bouncing, her brow knitted as her moans rise.

I grin down at her, using my grip on her ass to slam into her even harder, loving how each time she gets a little louder.

"You keep doing that, darling," I say, "and you'll make my brothers jealous." I delight at the idea, relishing the time I have with her right now, where I don't have to share.

"I," she breathes the word, moaning as I control her body, using her to squeeze out every drop of pleasure she possesses. "I can't help it," she says, her voice breaking off into a delightful little cry as her pussy clamps around my cock.

Fuck. Me.

"That's it," I say, shadows gathering around me, spearing for her. I use them to caress her breasts, her clit, and then slide one over her mouth.

Her eyes flare, fire sizzling in them at the shadow keeping her mouth closed.

"Be a good girl," I say, pumping into her with abandon. "Come for me again."

She arches as I increase my pace, my shadows working every other sensitive spot she has, plucking her like a fine instrument until—

A muffled moan slips through the shadow over her mouth, her back bowing, her body convulsing as her orgasm rips through her. Ice spiderwebs its way over the table, casting frosty snowflakes beneath her. Her heat pulses around my cock as I thrust into her, clenching me so good that I come right after her.

Our breathing is ragged as I draw her up, cradling her in my arms. She loops her arms around my neck, both of us looking down at the table, at the ice crystalizing over the All Plane emblem.

"Sorry—"

"An improvement," I cut her off, then kiss her. "One we should most certainly make permanent."

21

She smiles at me, our mouths a breath apart as I hold her against my chest. "Later," she says, then gently bites my lips.

"Later," I growl, then settle us into a chair and start all over again.

# 3

# TOR

"Our little wife will sink a dagger in Chador's skull if he continues to undermine us as the new kings," I say to Talon as we walk out of the monstrosity of a council room. It's perfect for a king in every way, built and outfitted for politics and plotting, but I prefer the sun on my skin and the wind on my face over stone walls and decorative tapestries. I need to be outside, fighting, fucking my mate, strategizing—anything to keep me busy.

"Chador is the least of our problems. We need to find Storm and River so we can prep to leave." Talon's jaw clenches as we exit the palace, rounding the corner and heading toward the sky ship bay.

Talon relies on his plans, his inventions. If he sits still for a second too long, he feels the weight of all the realms. He's always calculating, analyzing, preparing for every likely scenario. That's just how his mind works. It's the same reason he fought the draw to Cari when she first arrived. He couldn't see past the odds the king had sent her here to harm us.

And yeah, he'd been right, but he'd also been wrong.

Cari fell for us as deeply and profoundly as we had for her.

Watching Talon fight his need for our mate was laughable. I knew he'd relent. It was just a matter of time. Now I had the pleasure of watching him sweat while we all claimed our time with her, and he has to share. He *hates* sharing. If we weren't about to go to war, I'd delight in stealing Cari's attention from him any time she gave it to him, just to see how long he could withstand before trying to pummel me.

Talon had his plans, his inventions, and I had my brawls.

"You know River would rather join us in the upcoming fight than sit quietly and play politician," I say.

"Storm too," Talon says. "But we need them here. There's no one else we can trust."

I nod. "We'll have to entice them."

River likes his gadgets just as much as Talon, and is always upgrading his suits—specialized armor that allows him to shrink his size to near invisibility yet maintain his natural, All Plane-given strength. Training with him when he wasn't wearing one of his suits was hard enough—the male was light on his feet and hard as hell to hit—but when he wore the suit? Fuck, I always had to resort to hitting him with a bolt of lightning to short-circuit the suit's power in order to best him. I'm glad he's on our team, let alone my friend.

We slow to a halt outside the sky ship bay, easily spotting River and Storm's ship as it docks. "They're back," I say, clapping Talon between the shoulder blades. "Let's get down there and greet our friends."

Talon flashes me an incredulous look. No doubt my ease and joy in the moment is grating on his nerves, but I've always lived my life from second to second. I don't linger in the past and I don't agonize about the future. And at this moment, I refuse to let the upcoming war spoil the reunion of me and my best friend.

As we walk down the golden ramps lining the exterior of the palace, I notice a few of the palace staff staring at us, their foreheads pinched and their gazes narrowed. Sun damn us, they look as if we've come back from slaughtering a ship full of innocents.

Talon hardly notices, too wrapped up in the mission at hand.

But I see it, and heave a sigh.

It will take our people time to accept our new status, to accept a Shattered Isler as their queen. Cari is worthy of her title and she's every bit the warrior me and my brothers are. Her determination to stop her father on her own is impressive, I can't deny that. I couldn't have asked for a better mate. When we *do* find her father, she'll be the one to end his life.

"Tor," River says, crossing the distance between us and clasping my shoulder. His brown eyes are full of silent apologies. "We heard about your father," he says, shaking his head. "I'm sorry. We should've been here."

I swallow hard as the grief I've kept at bay rises and threatens to ruin my excitement over our reunion. I've managed to not think about my father's betrayal or his death for the entire morning, and here my best friend is, putting all that darkness out on display, forcing me to acknowledge it, work through it.

"Thank you," I finally say, gripping his shoulder back. He's wearing one of his signature suits, this one red and with more gadgets than should be possible to carry.

Storm isn't far behind River, greeting Talon in much the same way.

"Where were you two?" Talon asks as we walk up the ramp, heading toward the palace dining hall. "We could've used you when our father tried to imprison us and have us executed," he continues, his tone lighter than it's been all day.

"Your father ordered us to the Earth Realm under the guise that General Payne had been spotted torturing the locals," Storm says, his skin-tight silver shirt practically sparkling under the sun. It's damn near blinding, but the effect dulls as we walk inside the palace. It's a marvel to me he keeps pace with us at all, seeing as he's faster than any sky ship ever invented. The male could outrun a shooting star if he saw fit to do so.

We walk past the council room, toward the formal dining hall, and my ears pick up on the faint sounds of Cari's soft whimpers. Jealousy hits me like a punch to the gut, but it vanishes as quickly as it comes. I'm grateful Lock has found his match in Cari and good for him indulging while he can. If we didn't have other matters to attend to, I'd kick in the council room door and make him share.

"All bullshit, of course," River says, drawing me back to the present as the sounds in the council room fade, and we near the dining hall. "We were only there a couple of minutes before we realized the intel was false. Luckily, some local decided he had bigger balls than Storm, so it wasn't a total waste."

The formal dining room can fit a hundred people easily, but with the four of us and our collective powers, plus the massive feast spread across the main table, the room almost feels small.

Storm shrugs as we take a seat at the main table. "He challenged me," he says. "Thought he could use his earth magic to move him faster than I can run."

Talon rolls his eyes.

"He lost, of course," Storm says. "Then took a swing at me." He shrugs. "I tried my best to stay calm, but he was persistent. Didn't take long to put him in his place. It reminded me of the old days fighting those arrogant pricks on the Shattered Isle..." He stops short. "Shit, I guess I should watch what I say now that the Shattered Ilse princess is your wife."

Talon arches a brow at Storm. "She's the All Plane queen now," he says, and Storm dips his head in support.

"After the rumors we've heard about your new bride, Tor," River says, breaking the tension from where he sits next to me, pouring mead into all our glasses from the allotted pitcher. "I'm surprised to see you in the light of day and not between your mate's legs."

"Trust me, I'd rather be there. Lock is with her, so she's being taken care of."

Talon's brow furrows at the mention of Cari and Lock together, but he'll have to get used to it. She's more than enough mate to go around.

"I have to admit," Storm says, arms folded over his chest as he leans back in his chair. "I thought this was a ploy of your father's. Your marriage solely for the sake of conquering the

Shattered Isle." He presses his lips together, shaking his head. "We had no idea that he was planning to..." His voice trails off, like he can't even fathom how to speak the words of my father's betrayal.

"I should've seen it coming," Talon says, his shoulders tense.

I part my lips, prepared to tell him he can't see every single outcome, but he shakes it off and starts piling food on his plate, stealing the moment away.

"Who knew one Shattered Isle female would be a bonded mate to four stubborn princes of the All Plane," River says, lightening the mood. "She must possess some star magic that's made you all bend to her will," he jokes, slapping me on the back.

"You wish you could find someone who could handle all your bullshit," I say. "Jealousy doesn't suit you, my friend. Your time will come, probably when you least expect it." I nod to Talon after filling my plate. "Talon fought the bond the longest, but even he couldn't resist it in the end."

"I've met my match in every way," Talon admits as he digs into his food. "Cari has been underestimated her entire life, and I expect her to continue to surprise all of us as we navigate these uncharted waters together." He takes a few more bites, each of us doing the same. "As much as I want to keep talking about my mate," Talon says a few moments later. "We have more pressing matters to discuss now that you're both back."

"What can we do?" Storm asks after finishing his second leg of meat. His instant support sends a wave of calm over me, not that I ever doubted our friends, but then again, I'd never doubted my father either. I'd been blind to what his heart had twisted into, and it would take some time to get over that betrayal.

"You two have always been loyal," Talon says. "Our most trusted friends. We've been through wars and battles and political challenges," he continues, eyes bouncing between each of us. "I know Tor agrees on how much you've both meant to us over the years—"

"Cut the shit," River says. "We know you love us. Who wouldn't?" he jokes. "Tell us what you need."

"We need you both to stay in the All Plane," I say. "To maintain order while my brothers and our wife hunt down King Jerrick and put an end to his treachery for good."

"I thought we had him here?" River's brow furrows. "How did he get away? The All Plane palace and its sky ships are fortresses with every manner of spy drone and gadget Talon has ever invented. It's *impossible* to lose people!"

"We underestimated King Jerrick and our father," I say. "Sadly, there are still loyalists here to our father who assisted King Jerrick."

"He escaped," Talon says. "We were too focused on defeating our father."

"Cari ran after him," I explain. "Saw his sky ship take off. She wanted to fly after him, but we wouldn't let her."

"We had to claim our throne," Talon adds. "Had to claim it and *her* as our queen before someone tried to challenge us."

"Another mistake we made," I say, shaking my head. "Cari is a warrior. We should've let her chase after her father, maybe then we wouldn't be in the mess we're in now."

Talon cuts a glare at me. "If we let her do that, her position as queen would always be challenged. She'll have a hard enough time as it is. If her first act as queen was abandoning the All Plane before she'd even been crowned?" he scoffs. "The people would plaster that dishonor and shame upon her for centuries."

I swallow hard, knowing he's not wrong, but still regretting our choices all the same.

"You truly think she could've killed the Shattered Isle king?" River asks, eyes wide, curious.

"She's that powerful?" Storm asks.

A grin shapes my lips, pride swelling in my chest. "She would surprise even you, Storm." I wink at him. He's impossibly fast on the battlefield and we never have a fair shot to catch up to him. Even when we were younglings, he'd never slow down on our behalf. Talon eventually made a suit of armor with the ability to fly in order to make himself faster and give him a shot at winning against Storm. But Cari? I'd seen her power, felt it, tasted it. She could spear ice faster than he could outrun it. Lucky for him, he's on the right side of this war. *Our* side.

"Do you know where the Shattered Isle king is or where he's headed?" Storm asks.

"Regardless of where he is, is the chase worth leaving the safety of the All Plane to find him?" River tilts his head. "You are kings now. You have responsibilities you didn't have when you were princes."

"We know," Talon says, sighing. "And we had ships following him as soon as he escaped, but the ships lost him. He's taking forbidden routes."

My brother's tech is usually failsafe, so I know he's blaming himself for losing track of King Jerrick. I quash the urge to reach over the table and grasp his shoulder, knowing my sympathy would only spear his agitation. He's always taken our family's needs as his sole responsibility, carrying the weight of the entire All Plane on his shoulders despite how many times my brothers and I tell him he's not alone.

"We leave for the Shattered Isle in two days," Talon says.

"The king has to be retreating there. He knows he can't get caught out in the open with only a handful of guards to defend him. He needs his armies and his palace walls to protect him from us," I say.

"Cari has a friend who can help," Talon continues. "And we have a way of getting into the kingdom without being spotted."

"But the king hasn't reached the Shattered Isle yet," Storm says.

"No. We believe he's passing through the Stone Realm Territory. There are enough enemies to help him gather more supporters, but he's out of his element and will need to return to the Shattered Isle in order to keep his kingdom," I say.

The Stone Realm was once part of the Earth Realm, but was exiled from the mainland decades ago after the Stone Realm followers thought it would be a good idea to forge weapons and try to claim the All Plane throne. The Earth Realm followers are loyal to the All Plane, so they fought against them, casting them out. Without the Earth Realm's full support, the Stone Realm's agenda fell through, but they've always hated our kingdom. Sometimes, the Stone people will sneak into our realm, causing any havoc they can to create an upset among my people.

We finally signed a tentative peace treaty after decades of battles between our warriors and theirs. We don't cross each other's borders unless we're making an official declaration of war—which is why our sky ships lost King Jerrick when he crossed into their territory. They're ruthless, and likely wouldn't hesitate to help the Shattered Isle king if it brought them closer to ending our reign for good.

"We believe he wants a chance alone with his daughter as revenge for her betraying him. Cari wants the same chance. And afterward, she'll secure the future for both the All Plane and the Shattered Isle. She wants our kingdoms to unite, so she has to show her people the truth. King Jerrick knows his daughter and will use her idealistic nature to his advantage. We can't stop her from going, but our place in this is by her side," Talon says.

"With the changes our kingdom has witnessed these last few days, we want to ensure the safety of the All Plane," I say. "The people are expressing their fears with Cari as the new queen, and the last thing we want is to leave, but the Shattered Isle king has to be stopped. We trust you and Storm to ensure the All Plane's safety. Will you hold our throne for us?" I ask, sweat beading on the back of my neck. I'm itching to board a ship and make these plans a reality.

"You're starting to sound like Steel," River says, a smirk on his lips. "We don't need more pep talks and cheerleading." He extends his mug toward me.

I huff a laugh, clinking my mug against his before taking a drink.

"I've never met a woman worth going to war for," Storm says, arching a brow at Talon. "Is she really worth the blood that will spill?"

Talon and I share a look before we both nod.

"She's worth everything," I say.

# 4

# CARI

*L*ock's and my activities in the council room wore me out enough that he'd carried me to my bed and I slept half the day away. Which explains why it's now a sea of glittering darkness outside the palace, the stars visible but less vibrant here in the All Plane as I make my way through the palace.

I haven't seen any of my other husbands since the meeting this morning, and after the nap, I have a restless sense of urgency that is only fueled by a nervous energy I feel down my bond—from one mate in particular.

Following that sensation, I traipse through the palace hall-ways, admiring the artwork and décor and doing my best to ignore some of the spiteful looks I receive from the staff along the way. From the way some of the females look at me, I might as well be parading around in nothing but my skin—which I most certainly am not. I wear a loose pair of maroon cotton pants and a long-sleeved top with the All Plane emblem across the chest. The pajamas are soft and warm and fit my body like a glove. I no doubt have Steel to thank for

stocking my rooms here, likely before our bonding ceremony weeks ago. I smile, remembering how he'd stocked the
sky ship for our return here, and how thoughtful I'd found
my new husband when I'd expected a monster. I'll have to
hunt him down eventually, but right now, his bond is saying
he needs time to himself to think.

 I turn a corner, the nervous, unsettled energy magnifying as
I step through a cracked open door and into a massive room.

Clean, minimalistic cabinets cover the walls from floor to
ceiling, a concrete countertop splitting them in half, with all
manner of tools and gadgets scattered atop it. In the center
of the room is a large, round table, much like the one in the
council room, complete with holographic capabilities. The
bright blue lights above it illustrate a pathway in the sky I
recognize—the most direct route to my Shattered Isle.

And with his back to me, staring at that holographic map, is
Talon. The muscles in his back are tense and flex as he leans
over that table, his hands fisted the surface.

I eye the array of inventions that cover another table at the
farthest side of the room, admiring and wondering at all the
gears and spokes and flickering lights. The buzzing of electricity whirrs in a constant hum in the room, and the space
smells of leather and whiskey—like Talon.

Looking around the room, at the way Talon is so consumed
by his work that he doesn't even know I'm here, gives me
another little piece of him. The inventions, the technology
here, all are a testament to his genius, for certain, but there is
more to it than that alone.

I contemplate turning around and leaving him to his work,
but think better of it when a heavy sigh leaves his lips.

"This is incredible," I finally say, and Talon spins around, dark eyes wide as he takes me in, notes the All Plane clothes I wear.

"What is?" he asks.

I walk toward him, gesturing to the surrounding room. "This place," I say. "Your inventions." I eye one in particular, a work-in-progress metal glove, its wires poking out of a translucent covering. "Can you really make anything?"

Talon reaches into his pocket, withdrawing a thin black necklace and holding it before me. "I made something for you," he says.

I admire the piece. It's elegant and simple and made entirely of tiny stones that glitter beneath the lights in his workshop.

"You made this in the time I was gone today?" I ask as I reach for it.

"I work fast," he answers simply.

"Not always," I tease, and a small smirk shapes his lips.

I graze my finger across the center stone, which is light blue where the others are black—

The necklace vibrates beneath my touch, the soft whirring of electricity buzzing as it *shifts* before my eyes. No longer a necklace, but now a tiny, floating contraption no bigger than my hand. The stones that were once lined on the necklace are now gathered together in a sphere, all the black ones hugging the sky-blue piece, which rests in the center like an eye.

"What is it?" I ask after the shock of the transformation wears off.

Talon steps around the floating orb, his shoulder brushing mine as we both look at it. "That," he says, pointing toward it. "Is CB-1. Communication Bearer, unit one," he explains after I've arched a brow at him.

The orb's color flickers, almost like it blinks at us as it patiently waits.

Talon reaches for my hand, guiding it up and trailing my finger along the sky-blue stone. The orb immediately transforms back into the necklace.

"Some of my best AI work," he explains as he clasps the necklace around my neck, his fingers lingering on my skin and eliciting chills. "Imprinted with your first touch," he continues as I turn to face him, his eyes on where the blue stone rests at the base of my throat. "The unit will adapt and learn the longer you wear it. Your preferences, your needs. It's linked with my comms system and can send distress signals." He traces one of his fingers above it, teasing my collarbone. "But that's not the best part," he says, and an excitement churns in his eyes.

"It's not?" I say, absolutely flabbergasted. No one has ever made anything for me, let alone something as outstanding as what he's showing me.

Talon gives me a half smile, the only break in the serious expression he's worn for days now. "He has a brother."

I raise my brows. "Does he now?"

He nods. "Communication bearer, remember?" Talon turns, eyes on the 3D map still hovering over his table, and waves me over.

I step up to his side, our arms brushing, that bond of ours tightening between us with the physical touch.

"See that?" He points to a small, almost imperceptible ball of light moving through the sky on the map.

"Yes," I say, watching the tiny speck of light drift.

"That's the brother. CB-2. He'll allow communication to his owner whenever either of you like."

I furrow my brow, noting the path is heading straight toward my home. Emotion clogs my throat as I put the pieces together. There is only one person I'd want to be in communication with from my home…

"Gessi?" I ask, my voice a whisper as tears gather behind my eyes.

Talon dips his head. "CB-2 should reach her within the next few hours."

I open and close my mouth several times, the words tangling in my throat. "Talon," I finally manage to say before I throw my arms around his neck.

He catches me effortlessly, his arms snaking around my lower back, lifting me off my feet and hefting me to his level as I cling to him.

"I don't know how to thank you," I say. "I don't know what to say."

"You don't have to do either," he says, his cheek pressed against mine. He holds me a bit tighter, and I feel the anxiety skittering along our bond.

I draw back slightly, enough to where I can see his face. "What is it?" I ask, and then instantly cringe.

What a ridiculous question. War is at our doorstep, he's been crowned a king of the All Plane, and his father betrayed him, tried to kill him, and then died by the hands of one of his sons. Of course, that's what's bothering him.

"You don't have to answer that," I hurry to say. "I only meant, what can I do?"

He sighs, leaning his forehead against mine as he sets me back on my feet, then turns back toward the table. "I've been going over every route to the Shattered Isle known to exist," he says, waving with one hand toward the map. It instantly splinters into seven different routes, each one showing another section of the sky and the realms beneath it on the way. "Strategy and logic dictate that your father would take this one home," he says, illuminating the first path with another flick of his fingers. "But he didn't." He shakes his head, eying the other routes and motioning his hand to another path. "He was last sighted here."

I lean closer, examining the section of map he lit up. "I've never seen that on any map before," I say. Not even in my studies, which were extensive growing up. Father wanted me to know everything about the All Plane and the realms in between, but, then again, he'd also lied to me my entire life, so who's to say he showed me authentic maps?

"The Stone Realm," he says. "And you wouldn't. It was wiped off the map the minute the Earth Realm exiled them from their territory." He continues to explain the reasoning behind that, then turns around, leaning against the table and rubbing his palms over his face. "He's either holed up there, trying to recruit new followers to his cause, or he simply acquired another sky ship and is retreating back to the Isle. And if we breech the lines we've drawn between us and the Stone Realm, it will be an act of war on its own."

My eyes flicker from the map to Talon. He pinches the bridge of his nose, his shoulders hunched slightly, like a weight sits on top of them.

"Hey," I say, stepping in front of him, smoothing my hands over his cheeks, forcing him to look at me. "It'll be okay. We'll get him," I say. "With as little bloodshed as possible—"

"That's a fairytale," Talon cuts me off, pushing away from me and the table as he paces the space in front of it.

I furrow my brow.

"It is," he says, his voice tense. "You think there's an easy way out of this? Whatever choice I make, people will *die*. Good people and bad, but either way, all the deaths that pile up will be on my hands?"

Anger simmers beneath my skin, and I straighten my spine. "Your choice, your hands," I repeat, shaking my head. "Because you're the only king, right? You definitely don't have three brothers who bear the same responsibility, who are there for you to discuss and strategize and plan with. To *help* you. And you definitely don't have a queen ready and willing to do the same?"

Talon plants me with a sharp look. "That's not fair—"

"You're not being fair!" I fire back, stepping into his path so he stops pacing and faces me. "You are not in this alone, Talon."

"I am, though," he snaps. "I threw Lock into a cell I designed especially for him. My own brother. I'm the one who didn't see our father's treachery when it was sitting on my fucking hard drive, Cari." He flings an arm behind him, indicating the lit-up keyboards that seem never-ending on the other side of that table. "Me. I missed it. My mistakes. No one else's."

I swallow hard, breathing in through my nose and out through my mouth in an effort to not scream at him. "Look," I say, holding his fiery gaze. "You can blame yourself all you want. You can keep walking around like you have to carry the weight of this war on your own all you want. But I'm still going to be here. Fighting. For *you*. With you. And so will your brothers, if you just give them the chance."

Talon visibly swallows as he folds his arms over his chest.

I extend my arms out horizontally, a challenge or a comfort, whatever he needs to see.

"Are you going to sit here and drown yourself in blame, in trying to control every single thing to the point you drive yourself mad?" He flashes me a warning look at my tone, and it sends a flare of heat straight down the center of me. "Or are you going to let me help you? Let your brothers help you?"

A muscle in his jaw ticks, but I can see it there behind his dark eyes—the internal debate on actually letting me in, letting me carry some of this weight for him.

But when he's silent too long, I tilt my head at him. "What's it going to be, Talon?"

His arms fall to his sides, the iron walls over his eyes dropping along with them. "This is me, Cari," he says, his voice low and rough between us. "I'm the one who sees all the angles, the one who can predict the destruction seconds before it happens, but I can't always prevent it." He shakes his head. "Do you know how infuriating that is?" He paces again, raking his fingers through his hair. "And I can't help but feel if I work harder, look at the problem and the big picture long enough, I'll be able to stop all the bad before it happens. Before—"

41

I step into his path again, my fingers splayed on his hard chest. "You aren't the sun or the stars," I say. "You can't see the future, can't know everyone's fate. You *can't* put that kind of responsibility on yourself."

He grips my wrists, holding me against him as we stare each other down. "What if I can't stop doing that? What are you going to do?"

Heat streaks through my veins, a warm shiver trembling over my body at the amount of unrestrained need barreling down our bond.

"I'm going to stand by you," I say, stepping even closer so our bodies are flush. "Fight you every inch of the way until you let me help you."

"For how long?" he demands.

"Forever," I promise, our lips an inch apart. "I will weather whatever storm comes, Talon. I'm not going anywhere—"

His slants his mouth over mine, claiming my lips in a punishing kiss that only he's capable of. Sharp and searing. Hot and consuming. No soft teasing, no sweet flicks. Not with Talon. He's a constant burning flame, and he needs someone strong enough to withstand it, to not turn to ash if she gets too close.

Lucky for him, the stars bonded him to *me*.

I reach up and tangle my fingers into his dark hair, yanking him toward me, kissing him harder until a low groan slips from his lips.

"Cari," he breathes my name as he grips my ass, hefting me up and up until I have to lock my ankles around his back.

I keep kissing him, relishing the taste of him as he sweeps his tongue into my mouth, teasing the edges of my teeth and taking my breath away. He walks us to the nearest wall, pressing my spine against it for leverage as he frees one of his hands and plunges it beneath my shirt. He palms one of my breasts, pinching my nipple so hard I gasp before he quickly leans down, flicking his tongue over the small hurt.

I claw at his shirt, and he laughs as he gently sets me on my feet, allowing me the space to pull it over his head. I run my nails down his hard chest, over the ridges of his abdomen, and tug at the band of his pants. "You don't need these," I say.

"You're a pushy little mate, aren't you?" he teases, but does as I say, ridding himself of his pants in a blink.

"Your turn," he demands, and I grin as heat unfurls at my core as he stands there in all his magnificent confidence, knowing full well I won't deny him, won't fight him on this. Slowly, I peel the pajamas off, leaving them in a pool by my feet.

Talon's dark eyes rake over every inch of my skin, and awareness prickles where his gaze lingers. Our bond goes taut as he meets my eyes, and we hold each other there in some silent game of who will break first.

It's me.

I break first.

I reach for him, and he *lets* me spin him until his back is against the wall. I hold his gaze as I drop to my knees before him, wrapping my fingers around his hard cock, stroking the thick shaft as I flick my tongue over the head.

"Fuck, Cari," he groans, his head dropping back against the wall.

I suck him into my mouth, my jaw straining at the sheer size of him, but my heart racing at the sensation of him filling me in this way. I bob up and down, swirling my tongue around him while I continue to stroke him with my hand.

Talon's fingers sink into the strands of my hair, fisting it as I continue to take him in my mouth. I slide my free hand over his massive thigh, digging my nails in before gripping his hip and moving it toward me so he's thrusting deeper.

The grip on my hair tightens, the muscles in his body flexing as I up my pace. He groans, and I swear I feel those vibrations all the way down to my heat. Making this powerful, intelligent male growl is a high I never knew existed. A power I never knew I needed.

I flick my gaze up to his, taking him in my mouth as far as possible before pulling back to the tip and doing it again. There is nothing but fire in his eyes as he watches me, and then I can't help but smirk as I draw my power to my lips, chilling my mouth enough to make him hiss. The searing hot and icy cool combination makes his eyes roll back in his head, and a drop of precome slides along my tongue.

"Cari," he warns as I alternate between stroking and sucking, swirling and teasing.

The sound of my name on his tongue has me shifting my thighs together, needing friction to ease the ache there. I drag my teeth over his shaft in the lightest of grazes before swirling a bit of cold around him again.

He yanks on my hair, just enough that I'm looking up at him again, and I dig my nails into his hip, returning the pleasurable bite of pain.

"You're going to take it," he demands, his voice strained from what I'm doing to him. He cocks a brow at me. "You're going to take all of it, understand?" He thrusts into my mouth on his own, and I moan from the thrill that shoots down my spine as he takes control, using his grip on my hair and his hips to take what he needs, to give himself over to me in every way possible.

I swirl my power in my mouth, creating a spiral of slick ice and heat, and he groans as he comes. I swallow him down, and he gently pulls on my hair until his cock comes out of my mouth with a satisfying pop. He smooths a thumb over my swollen lips, and pure satisfaction and love ripples down our bond.

"My turn," he growls the words, and in seconds, I'm on my back, the cold concrete floor pressing against my overheated skin.

Talon grips my knees, hauling them apart before lowering his head between my thighs, plunging his tongue inside my heat.

"Mmm," he moans, drawing back enough to look at me. "You're already so wet for me."

I arch into his mouth as he licks me again, fucking me with his tongue like he just fucked my mouth. There is no teasing with Talon, no drawn out torture, not tonight. Tonight there is nothing but frenzied hunger and pent-up energy and I'm more than happy to be the one he takes it out on.

He eats at me so fast and so hard my orgasm is already there, right on the cusp and all it takes is one graze of his teeth over that swollen bundle of nerves—

"Talon!" I gasp as my orgasm rips through me, my thighs clenching around his head as he continues to lick me through it. I ride his mouth, chasing my pleasure all the way into a second one before he gently draws away, grinning down at me with nothing but pure male confidence on his face.

Talon slides his hands beneath my ass, hefting me up so I'm chest to chest with him, my thighs on either side of his hips, his hard cock teasing my slick, swollen heat.

And then he lets go, and I sink fully atop him in one fast motion that has fire licking up my spine.

He captures my mouth, holding me flush against him as he thrusts into me from below. I clench my thighs, taking the reins as I move up and down on him, digging my nails into his shoulders as I ride him.

"Fuck, Cari," Talon growls as I completely take control, riding him hard, relishing the bite of pain from the size of him as I take him at this angle.

I playfully bite his lips, and he smacks my ass, causing me to rock against him harder, faster. So fast I can barely catch my breath. So hard I can't think around the pleasure building and climbing inside me. Our bond stretches taut, nothing but fire and strength spiraling around it as we consume each other.

Everything inside me narrows to the feel of losing myself so entirely in this male, to the way he fills every inch of my soul, the way I can't breathe around how fucking fantastic he feels. "Talon," I moan his name, gripping his hair as I rock against him.

"You feel that?" Talon says, breathless as he hardens inside me another degree. He thrusts upward, over and over again, his fingers clenching my hips as he drives into me. "You feel what you do to me?"

Each thrust pushes me toward that sweet edge, and when he slips his hand between us, rolling his fingers over my clit, I shatter completely. My thighs tremble as I clench around his cock, my entire body convulsing from the intensity of my orgasm. Talon pistons his hips, thrusting into me hard and fast before he follows me over the edge with a groan.

Our breathing is ragged as we cling to each to other, my forehead pressed against his, our bodies slick with sweat as we come down.

I kiss him happily, shifting to lean my head against his shoulder, the angle showing me something in his workshop I hadn't seen before. I draw back to look at him, motioning to the small drones positioned in the ceiling corners of his room.

"Are those camera drones?" I ask.

Talon nods, catching his breath. "I'll delete the footage," he assures me.

I purse my lips, then shrug. "Or you could keep it," I practically purr, and his eyes widen as he stares down at me.

"Surprising, devious little mate," he says before claiming my mouth.

# 5

# CARI

*I*t took a few hours to convince Talon to get some sleep—and by convincing, I mean wearing him out so thoroughly he had little choice.

Heat simmered beneath my skin, my body still buzzing from what we'd done to each other in his workshop. I bit back a smile as I walked into my room in the palace—which was three times the size it had been on the sky ship. My mates graciously designated a space that was solely mine—a place for the extensive wardrobe they bought me, a bathing chamber big enough for five, and a reading area complete with a mini library. They wanted me to have the luxury of recharging or have alone time, if that's what I wished, though they'd each given me a standing invitation to sleep in their quarters whenever I liked.

Truly, I might be the most spoiled queen in all the realms.

*The only queen in all the realms,* my voice echoes inside my mind, and I flinched at the weight of that reality. I haven't had a second to process my new role and the responsibilities that came with it. But I will. Soon. After I finish what I started with my traitor of a father.

And while I knew I should practice what I preach and go to bed to prepare for the upcoming journey we had ahead of us, there's one thing I simply have to do before I rest.

I unclasp the necklace Talon made me, brushing my finger over the sky-blue stone. CB-1 whirs to life, hovering at my eye level as I sink onto the edge of my bed. A light shimmers from beneath the blue eye, the dark stones around it opening and closing randomly as if blinking at me. I chuckle, antici-pation filling my chest as I say, "Connect with CB-2, please."

CB-1 shudders a little where he hovers, a soft chiming sound murmuring as a blue light snakes out from his center, illumi-nating the area on the end table next to my bed. A more gentle ray of light scans my body, the little robot bobbing up and down in the air slightly, almost looking as excited as I feel.

"Cari?" Gessi's voice echoes from CB-1 a second before the blue light shapes her image—a miniature Gessi sits on my end table, confusion flickering in her hazel eyes.

She wears the sleeveless gown of a Shattered Isle hand-maiden, one I know is black and sparkling like stars, the fabric making her natural jade skin shimmer. But, the light from CB-1 makes her look as cobalt as I am, as if we truly are the sisters we've always behaved as.

My father had told me he'd saved Gessi from the Earth Realm during The Great War after the All Plane king had slaughtered her family. We'd been infants and had grown up together on my Isle, Gessi appointed as the princess's hand-maiden—but in truth, she was the sister I'd never had.

Guilt slithers over my heart and my stomach sinks as I try to find the words to speak to her. Steel had told me the truth of the battle between my father and the Earth Realm—he hadn't saved anyone, but merely stolen Gessi, along with a handful of other young innocents, and taken them as captives to be raised under his reign.

"*Gessi*," I blurt out her name, emotion clogging my throat. My heart expands at the sight of her, at the sound of her voice. It's only been a few weeks, but I've missed her every single day. We were inseparable on my island, and now that I know the truth of my father's nature, I can't stand the thought of her there without my protection.

"This contraption just showed up a few minutes ago," she says, shock coloring her features. "It flew through the air and wrapped around my neck," she continues, her fingers tracing her collarbone as she speaks. "I thought it was a weapon sent to kill me." She laughs then, and I can't help but join her—picturing a necklace flying through the air and wrapping around her throat is truly quite funny. "Thank the stars, it wasn't."

"I didn't know it was coming for you," I say, reality grounding me to the present. "Talon, one of my mates, made these so we could communicate."

"So, they do still live. The rumors are true." Gessi smiles, but I know her well enough to spot the cracks. She blinks a few times, shaking off the laughter like she'd forgotten where she was for a moment. "Cari," she says, her voice grave as her eyes scan something around her I can't see. "I don't have much time."

I scoot closer to the light, to her. "What's happening there? Has my father already returned?"

She shakes her head. "He left General Payne in charge when he departed, not two hours after you boarded the sky ship with your new husbands."

"He beat us here," I hurry to say. "He and the All Plane king had made a deal—"

"I've heard the whispers," she says. "Crane wouldn't say much, but he told me enough to understand why the Isle is in revolt."

My lips part, shock rattling through me. Crane has been one of my father's guards for as long as I can remember, the same age as Gessi and me. He's climbed the ranks over the years, assigned as General Payne's right-hand watchdog. Nothing gets by him, and while I hope he's still the semi-friendly guard I remember, ever since learning the truth about my father, I'm doubting everyone I grew up with. Except Gessi. I know her like I know my own heart—ours is a bond that can't be broken or scarred, regardless of time or distance.

"What do you mean revolt?" I ask.

Her eyes dart behind me, though I know she isn't looking at my quarters, but something there I can't see. "News has spread about the All Plane king's death and your father's hand in it. They say he planned it all and is now waiting to strike the new kings down and take all the realms for himself."

I blow out a breath, adrenaline coursing through my veins.

"Leaving General Payne in charge didn't sit well with some of our people, naturally," she says, shaking her head. "There are whispers of some of the outer villages across the Isle taking up arms and joining forces. General Payne is wiping them out as fast as the rumors arise, even without proof.

Anyone who even glances at him in a way he doesn't like is subject to imprisonment, torture, and then death without a trial."

Acid climbs up my throat.

"He's formed a hunting unit," she continues, her lip curling. "Crane won't even dare speak to me anymore." She sighs. "I've tried asking what the general is forcing him to do on these expeditions..." Her eyes go distant for a moment, some unseen horror flickering there. "He comes back looking so..." She frowns, refocusing on me. "And it's getting worse. There are rebels in the royal city, inside our palace walls. At least, what the general calls rebels, which equates to anyone who stands up to him. Anyone who openly challenges his gruesome methods of ruling or any who expresses their interest in hearing what the new All Plane kings have to offer in terms of peace between our realms." She sucks in a sharp breath. "He slaughtered a mother in the street last night because she was overheard saying she thought the princes were kind enough when they were here for your wedding ceremony and that if they made her princess happy, then she would stand behind their rule."

I cover my gasp with my hand, my heart cracking. That woman died because of me, because she supported my love of the princes. No doubt stories had trickled back to the Isle about our journey—I was seen countless times laughing and dancing and kissing my husbands in public throughout each of the realms. Night damn me, her blood is on my hands, the blood of any innocent—

"Don't do that," Gessi whisper-hisses, chiding me. "You are not to blame and we don't have time to wallow right now. We'll do that after all this is over. I'm sure the palace has an excellent place for us to wallow for a week, but for now, we have only minutes."

I nod, focusing. "I'm coming to get you—"

"You absolutely are not coming to get me," she cuts me off, and I gape at her. "Your father ordered me to the general's side before he left."

"Stars save us," I say, shaking my head. My best friend under the rule of General Payne? I can think of no worse monster to be beholden to, save for my father. "All the more reason I need to come and get you."

"I've fared fine on my own these last few weeks," she says, though she shudders as an untold story plays across her eyes. "And this position is priceless." Her eyebrows raise, begging me to see the advantage, but I can't. She's the only genuine family I have besides my mates. How can she expect me to leave her at the mercy of that evil piece of shit? "I bring him his meals," she continues, as if she can't see the panic on my face. "His drinks. He has me take notes at his private meetings and sends me on errands to deliver messages to people in our royal city." She tilts her head at my silence. "Don't you see what this means? You have a shadow spy in your arsenal now, my queen," she whispers the title, something like pride shaping her smile.

"You are my best friend," I correct her. "You do not work for me—"

"You can't stop me," she says with challenging smirk on her lips as if we're kids again, playing with earth and ice and seeing who can make the best playhouse on the beach of our midnight ocean. "And with this gadget, I can easily relay important information to you so you can put an end to this. It's a win-win."

I purse my lips at her. "And when he catches you? When one of the guards overhears you telling me something? Then what?" A knot forms in my throat. "Who wins if you're thrown into a cell and tortured?" Icy panic claws up my spine.

Not her.

Never her.

Gessi rolls her eyes, as if I've said something completely ridiculous. "Do you seriously underestimate me that much? Maybe I really was just a silly handmaiden to you all those years—"

"Don't you dare!" I snap, and Gessi laughs at the attitude in my voice. I shake my head, unable to not laugh with her. She knows me, knows how to bait me into a fight or calm me and prevent one from happening. "Gess," I plead. "I can't risk you."

"Good thing you're not the one risking me then," she says, shrugging. "I can do this. You know how well I can play roles. Your own father never knew about half the things we did as younglings, right? Because the dutiful handmaiden answered to him and him alone and would never jeopardize the integrity of his princess." She grins, and I shake my head. "They'll never know. And with your father still in where-abouts unknown, and the general wreaking havoc here, someone has to help. I've always believed you were the change our world needed," she says, and I choke on tears. "And any way I can help you create that change, I will. No arguments."

I take a deep breath, knowing I wouldn't allow anyone else to sway me either—not away from my mission, not away from my mates, not away from doing what's right. "How did I get so lucky?" I ask. "Having a best friend like you?"

"With what's come to light about your father, the truth separating our people, lucky is the last thing I'd call you."

I swallow hard. "It's true," I say. "What they're saying. My father...he lied to me, to all of us."

"We'll have to unpack that another time," Gessi says. "The general's wine isn't going to pour itself." She glances over her shoulder, then back at me. "Tell me they're being good to you? Or shall we add them to the list of beings who need to die before this war is done?"

A broken, half-sob, half-laugh leaves my lips. "I miss you," I say, unable to keep the emotion from my voice. "And they're my mates," I explain. "My true, bonded mates. They're everything."

Gessi grins, nodding. "Good. But mates or no, if any of them hurts you, I'll bury them so far in the ground they'll forget what the sun looks like."

"I love you."

"I love you more," she says. "I'll reach out when I can."

"Okay," I say. "The hunt for my father begins tomorrow."

"Stay sharp," she says. "And use your star-blessed gifts to end this, Cari."

"I will."

We stare at each other for a few more seconds before Gessi waves her hand and her image dissolves before my eyes.

My shoulders hunch as a sob tears through me, a well of emotion cascading out too forcefully for me to hold back.

My Isle is suffering, my best friend is working under the vilest creature I've ever known, and my father is still out there somewhere, free and plotting and doing stars know what.

In the middle of it all, the realms are restless as the All Plane is in transition with new kings and a Shattered Isle queen. And if we're not careful, if we don't ensure those who are loyal to us remain, and help bring the realms together, the war between us could change our world entirely.

CB-1 hovers a little closer, tucking himself in the crook of my neck, a warmth buzzing from inside his spherical form. And I can't help but laugh through my tears as I reach up and pat the little orb, as if he somehow knew I needed some warm comfort when the icy panic inside me overwhelming.

Talon said the little robot would adapt to my needs, learn what I like…

I shift on the bed, moving toward my pillows and tucking myself under the covers. CB-1 follows me, hovering a short distance away. "Can you play music?" I ask, feeling slightly mad speaking to a robot.

CB-1 bobs up and down.

"Something to help me sleep?" It's the last thing I want to do, but I know I need to be at my strongest if I'm going to stand a chance against my father.

The little orb settles onto the pillow next to me, and soft, soothing music begins to play—melodies with strings and flutes and all the peaceful notes I need to drift to sleep, like I'm floating in one of the midnight ocean currents on my Isle.

I spiral away from this reality and sink into dreams of blood and revenge.

# 6

# CARI

*B*eams of buttery sunlight cast the smaller ship—more discreet than the palace in the sky—in a glistening, golden glow. Talon and Tor walk with me, carrying my single bag of luggage toward the ship that is fully stocked for our journey. This ship is for stealth and combat missions and is a favorite of Tor's best friend, River, or so he'd told me.

"Why aren't we taking one of your ships again?" I ask Talon as we near the loading bridge. Talon is known for outfitting his ships with all manner of inventions and I know we'll need all the help we can get when it comes to defeating my father. "This one looks…worn," I say, eying the scorch marks along its side, no doubt from an attack or two.

"Are you bashing Anthony?" a masculine voice calls moments before he walks out from beneath the ship hovering in the bay. He's tall, with black hair and hazel eyes that look like pine and amber in this light. A light dusting of a beard shadows his strong jaw and he wears a red and black suit that forms to his muscular body, buckles and straps holding weapons and flickering gadgets across his broad chest.

"Who's Anthony?" I ask as Tor embraces the man.

The man gestures behind him as he walks with Tor to stop before me. "My ship," he says. "He may not look like much, but he's far superior to whatever monstrosity Talon has in his holdings." He casts Talon a smirk, and Talon rolls his eyes.

"We're taking River's ship because mine are too well-known throughout the realms. We don't want to give your father the benefit of spotting us before we get to him," Talon explains. "Traveling in this hunk of junk, we'll easily be mistaken for common smugglers."

River waves his hands mockingly while rolling his eyes. "I'm Talon, too famous to take my own ships anywhere. Please, no pictures today, I'm exhausted from being a king and getting whatever I want—"

A laugh tears from my lips unexpectedly at River's impression, and Talon cuts me a teasing glare that promises punishment for laughing at his joke, which only makes me laugh harder.

"Really though," River says, dipping slightly in a bow that makes me shift nervously on my feet. I'm in discreet fighting leathers and an oversized white tunic, my long dark hair hanging in messy waves over my shoulders—I'm hardly wearing a crown that would warrant this kind of greeting. "Anthony is a solid ship. He'll get you where you need to go and is particularly good about getting into and out of small spaces. Perfect for what you're setting out to do." He flashes Tor a sympathetic look, then arches a brow at him. "Sure I can't tag along?"

Tor claps him on the back, shaking his head. "Next time," he says, and River nods.

The friendship between the two is effortless, the kind of banter and silent support that makes me miss Gessi all the more. She's risking her life to aid us in this upcoming mission, and while I'd love to have her at my side—as River is offering to be at Tor's—I know she has the right to make her own choices about her role in this war.

River extends his hand toward me, and I take it. "It's good to finally meet you," he says, nodding toward Tor. "This one hasn't been able to shut up about you. Is it true you can manipulate ice or is he just boasting again?"

I smirk at him, then coat my hand in a thin layer of ice so quickly he jerks his hand back. "Nice," he says, shaking out his hand. "Can you do me a favor?" he asks.

"What—"

"You've known her all of two minutes and already you're begging for handouts? Typical," another masculine voice cuts me off. This one wears a skin-tight silver shirt, the sun's beams reflecting off it and making his muscles look like welded metal. He shakes his head, his light brown hair shaking in messy waves atop his head, and embraces Talon in the same way River embraced Tor moments ago. "The council meeting went fine, by the way," he says, glaring at River.

River puts his hands on his chest in an innocent gesture. "What? I was there."

"Not in the way that counted," the male says.

River shrugs. "I like listening when no one thinks I'm there," he says. "I learn more that way, Storm. You know that."

Storm. So this is Talon's best friend. I blow out a breath, shaking my head as I examine the two. They certainly make them strong and handsome in the All Plane. Truly, these two are as appetizing as any of my mates, but of course, they don't hold a lick of my attention in any other way than intrigue.

"This was an official All Plane council meeting acknowledging our proxy by the kings' rule," Storm says. "Not some back-tavern poker game where you learn what cards your opponents have. You should've shown face."

River gapes at him, then flashes me an innocent grin. "Don't listen to him, my queen, I'm an honorable—"

"Thief," Tor cuts him off, laughing. "Don't hide who you are from her," he warns. "She'll figure you out either way, and lying isn't the way to earn her trust."

I snort a laugh. "That can be said for most females, River," I say easily. "Take note." I wink, and River grins at me.

"I like this one," River says.

"Yeah," Talon says, shrugging. "She's not bad."

I playfully smack his chest, but he captures my wrist, hauling me closer to him and lowering his voice between the two of us. "Bad girl," he teases.

Warm shivers dance down the center of me, but I pull my hand away, determined to keep my head as we prepare for our journey.

"Where is Steel?" I ask, feeling like a piece of me has been missing since he left the council room yesterday morning. I haven't seen him since, and it's unsettling to say the least.

"He'll be here," Lock's voice is at my ear, startling me enough that I whirl around. Lock steps out of a bulk of shadows. "Shortly, darling," he adds, grinning like a cat at the way he'd snuck up on me.

I turn back to face our little gathering. Lock absently trails his fingers over my shoulders and down my spine.

River and Storm narrow their gazes, each taking a step closer to Tor and Talon, almost as if it's an instinct to protect their friends from Lock. Something twists in my chest, and I fix a glare on both of them for their reaction.

"Lock," River is the first to break, shaking off the suspicious look and earning a modicum of my respect back.

"Lakewater," Lock says, and I bite my lip, shaking my head as I silently chide him for the jab.

River rolls his eyes, taking it in stride. "That never gets old, Keyhole." He laughs, and the tension finally breaks between them as Lock laughs too.

Okay, so maybe I like the funny one.

I glance at Storm, who stands near Talon. They're both wearing similar looks of strain and seriousness, and I sigh. Talon has made peace with his brother, but that doesn't mean his friends will so quickly. And I can't really blame Storm, seeing as how I believed Lock to be a dangerous murderer on the run before I actually got to know him. It just infuriates me that Lock isn't given that chance—so many are too afraid to get close to him to see how incredible he is.

Tor grabs our bags and, with River's help, they board the ship to store them.

Silence settles heavily between the four of us, and I'm just about to break it when I *feel* him. The bond between us flares inside me, tingling with awareness, and I spin around, brushing past Lock.

"Steel," I say, hurrying to close the distance between us and throwing my arms around his neck.

He catches me easily, holding me to him with one arm, his cheek pressed against mine. "I'm sorry I didn't come to you last night," he whispers in my ear. "I needed time to think."

"Don't apologize," I say, pulling out of his embrace as he sets me on my feet. I look up at him, the final pieces of my soul clicking together now that all my mates are nearby. "I understand. I just missed you."

He grins down at me, his crystal blue eyes lighting up in that way they do that steals my breath. Smoothing a hand over my cheek, he asks, "Do you have everything you need?"

My heart expands as I nod. Steel, the heart of my mates, the one who will always ensure I'm warm, I'm fed, I'm safe.

We head toward the ship, where Storm eyes Steel's bag. "You need me to get that for you, my king?" He bows at the waist with a gleam in his eye that speaks to years of teasing between them.

"I can manage on my own, thanks," Steel says with equal charm.

"Are you sure, brother?" Lock says from where he leans against the ship's loading bridge. "It looks heavy."

"Heavy mission, heavy bag," Steel says by way of explanation, and the levity of the moment bursts.

Lock straightens, dips his head, then heads up the loading bridge and into the ship, his long hunter green coat flaring behind him. Talon motions to Storm and they share a silent goodbye before Talon boards the ship too. Steel leads the way, me following at his side before Storm reaches out, stopping me with a pleading look in his eyes.

"May I beg a favor, my queen?" Storm asks, all earlier cockiness set aside for loyal submission.

Interesting. "Weren't you giving River hell over that just a moment ago?" I tilt my head.

He clears his throat. "Yes, but he's not listening now. And neither is Talon."

"All right, what is it?"

"Don't let Talon shoulder this burden alone. Don't let him fall on the sword for the sake of the rest of us," he continues, his brow furrowed. "I'm normally there to watch his back, and I'm happy to stay here and make sure your kingdom is safe for when you return, but if you could make sure my best friend comes back in one piece, I'll owe you."

I swallow hard, noting the loyalty to Talon, and absorb it. I'm wary of new people—a byproduct of my upbringing—but he seems genuine, if not this side of arrogant.

"He's my mate," I say matter of factly as I walk up the landing bridge. "If anyone wants to destroy him—*including* himself," I call over my shoulder, "they'll have to go through me." I smile and wink at him, and he dips his head to me as I board the ship.

My mates are standing in what I can only call a gathering area at the top of the loading bridge. Silver, cushioned benches are attached to the walls, cabinets and compartments strewn above them, holding who knows what.

River laughs at something Tor says, then points to the bridge. "I'll see you on the other side, my friend," he says, then stops before me. "Do me a solid, your highness," he starts, and I smirk, thinking he's going to ask the same of me as Storm did. "Take care of my baby."

"You call Tor your baby?" I arch a brow at my mate, who shakes his head.

"What?" River scrunches his brow. "No, he's fine. I mean Anthony. My *ship* is my baby."

I laugh, then nod to him. "I'll do my best," I call to him as he walks down the bridge.

"So," I say, turning back to my mates now that we're alone. "I spoke to Gessi last—"

A loud *thunk* cuts off my words. The ship bobs up and down as if something slammed onto the roof.

"For sun's sake, we haven't even taken off yet," Tor grumbles, lightning crackling between his fingers. "Are we under attack already?" He rushes out of the ship, Steel on his heels, Talon a second behind.

Lock remains seated on one of the silver benches, one ankle over his knee as he thumbs through a tablet.

"Aren't you coming?" I ask, heart racing as I head down the bridge.

"Oh, no, darling," he says, flashing me a smirk. "There is no threat." He tilts his head, pursing his lips. "Well, not now at least."

I give him a puzzling look, leaving him behind as I race out of the ship, ice daggers manifesting in my hands—

I crash into Tor's muscular back, and he steadies me with one massive arm before I can topple over.

"False alarm, little wife," he says, turning around and pointing to the roof of the ship.

I blink the stars out of my eyes from crashing into him, little currents of electricity raising the hairs on the back of my neck and making my body perk up in other ways that are not really beneficial for battle.

I follow where he points, noting River, Talon, and Storm glaring up in the same direction.

"You didn't think you were leaving without me, did you?" the male—who is standing on the roof of the sky ship—asks.

The male leaps from the roof, landing with preternatural grace in front of Steel. He's wearing a black shirt with only one sleeve. His left arm is bare, no doubt to show off the sleeve of silver star tattoos he has covering his arm from shoulder to fingers. A single red star is etched into the artwork on his skin, cords of muscle rippling beneath as he stands before Steel. The slight breeze whisks back his shoulder-length black hair, revealing arctic-blue eyes that are as chilling as the ice in my veins.

Instinctively, I move to Steel's side, daggers still in hand, sizing up the male even as I have to look *up* to him since he matches Steel's height.

"We already talked about this," Steel says, his tone low and warning yet somehow…gentle.

I glance between the two, noting the way Steel is relaxed—no fear ripples down our bond.

"Blaize," I whisper the name, and the male's eyes cut down to mine.

"This her?" he asks Steel, dismissing me with a look as he focuses on his friend.

"Your queen," Steel says. "Cari."

Blaize looks to me again, eyes raking up and down my body —not in a sexual way, but more an ascertaining-my-power way.

I do the same to him, opening my senses to the power I can feel rolling off his body in waves. He's got loads of it, that's for sure, but my eyes keep going back to his left arm. "I like your tattoos," I finally say, because it's the truth.

Something softens in him as he shifts on his feet, just slightly, to glance down at it. "I wanted to piss off Augustus," he says, and I arch a brow at how informally he refers to the past All Plane king. Blaize shrugs. "Guy didn't like stars, plus, he was a prick."

"Watch your fucking mouth," Talon snaps behind us, and I jolt a little at the harshness in his tone. My soul remembers the times he's used that tone on me, and I'm not keen to hear it again.

Blaize tilts his head, those arctic eyes darkening a degree as he meets Talon's gaze, then dismisses him just as easily and looks at Steel. "You're not going without me," he says. "I have every right to fight for your kingdom as she does," he motions to me, and I straighten.

"It's not just *his* kingdom," Tor says, arms crossed over his broad chest, lightning flashing in his eyes.

Blaize doesn't even look at him as he responds, "He's the only one I trust, so until you assholes earn it, it's his kingdom I'll serve." He glances down at me. "Goes for you too."

I tip my chin, silently observing the rogue Talon and Tor spoke of yesterday.

"I told you yesterday," Steel says, lowering his voice as if there is any semblance of privacy here. "I don't need the pissing matches between you and Talon distracting me. It would take us twice as long to achieve our mission because you two would no doubt be trying to rip each other's throats out every chance you got."

Blaize huffs a laugh at that, and I slowly back away, sensing the tension in Steel. He needs space, so I urge Talon and Tor back onto the ship. They go reluctantly after some silent looks from me, but I linger at the base of the ship, just in case Steel needs me. He's stronger than any male I've ever known, but I know better than anyone that those closest to us have the power to hurt us most. Not that I sense that from Blaize with the fierce determination he has to go on this mission with Steel, but you can never be too careful.

Again, my eyes linger on that arm, the mostly silver ink separated by thin lines of black, but that red star...it's striking and such a *fuck you* to the previous All Plane king who claimed star worshipers were maddened fools who would just as likely kill you as speak to you. And this one permanently inks one on his arm—

"Careful, darling," Lock says from directly behind me.

I look up at him over my shoulder, and he nods toward where Blaize and Steel are still speaking in hushed tones.

"Stare at him that way for too long and I might have to strangle him on principle," he whispers the words, his lips grazing the shell of my ear, and I arch back against him before spinning around to face him.

"Lock," I chide him, reaching up to loop my arms around his neck. I have to stand on my tiptoes to manage to move. "I didn't know you were capable of jealousy," I tease.

He snakes his arms around my lower back, tucking me tight against him. "You have no idea what I'm capable of when it comes to keeping my mate's attention."

My skin warms, something deep inside me tightening into a knot only he can unravel. "And yet," I say, keeping up the little game. "You aren't jealous of your brothers."

He lowers his head, brushing his lips over mine in a too-light kiss. "They're your mates too," he says. "It's only fair. But him?" His blue-green eyes flash behind us to Blaize. "He's no one's mate."

Something about the way he says that makes me sad, as if, since finding my mates, I want everyone to experience the love and joy that comes with it. I slide my fingers into the strands of Lock's black hair, relishing the silky feel. "I like his tattoos, Lock," I say with all seriousness. "That doesn't mean I want to ride him."

Fire flashes in Lock's eyes as he grins down at me. "I love it when you speak like that," he says, and my toes curl in my boots from the way he holds me. It's as if we're the only two beings in existence with all the time in the world to explore and tease and play.

But we're not.

And we have a mission.

I part my lips, but Lock slants his mouth over mine, stealing my words with a kiss before drawing back.

"As much as I love watching you two fight," Lock calls over to Steel and Blaize. "We're on a schedule. People to hunt, kings to kill."

Blaize affords Lock the same glare he's given pretty much everyone but Steel, and I can't help but wonder what his life has been like to turn him into the jaded, arrogant male he is. Not to mention how he and Steel became friends...*That* story, I'm dying to hear.

"I'm coming," Steel says, his tone laced with power and confidence, the kind that makes you feel comfortable following him into battle, and proud to fight at his back.

"Come, darling," Lock says, tugging me toward the ship. "Steel can manage against Blaize on his own."

Reluctantly, I follow Lock onto the ship, taking a seat next to him, Tor on my other side as Talon sets our coordinates in the ship's cockpit.

It's another thirty minutes before Steel boards, and I look behind him, half expecting him to have lost the battle with Blaize and find him following Steel onto the ship, but the path is empty, and the bridge seals as soon as Steel boards.

Steel sinks onto a bench across from us, raking a hand through his hair before he leans against a round table next to him. His sky-blue eyes are heavy, and the sense of regret that ripples down our bond has me rising from my seat, walking on shaky feet as the ship takes flight, and sitting down next to him.

I don't say anything, and he doesn't either, but I take his hand, interlocking our fingers in a silent attempt to siphon off some of the pain lingering in his eyes. Whatever happened between Blaize and Steel's brothers *hurts* him, and yet, Steel defended him against Talon yesterday, which speaks more to Blaize's true character than Steel's.

And I can't help but wonder if Steel would be happier if Blaize would've ignored his orders to stay behind.

"Tell me that's just fog," I say as Talon guides the ship above the landing strip in the Earth Realm. My gut clenches, knowing it's definitely not fog.

"Smoke," Talon says, his tone sharp. His hands flutter over the control panel, clicking and pushing buttons and switches as we wade through the thick slate smoke.

I'm out of the cockpit before he lands, heading for the loading bridge. Adrenaline courses through my veins as Tor, Lock, and Cari are on their feet in seconds from where they've been lounging in the gathering area.

"Trouble, brother?" Tor asks from where he stands at my right.

"Smoke," I say. "Could be natural fires from the Earth Realm's quarterly burn sessions, but something is off about it. No one responded to Talon when he tried to request authorization to land."

Cari steps up to my left, her eyes flickering with scenarios and the stress of each playing across her features. The once comfortable warm room drops in temperature, the bite of cold nipping at us all.

"Lock," I say, turning around to face him as the sky ship whirrs with the sound of docking. "Can you hear anything? Sense anything from the citizens here?"

Lock closes his eyes, arms calmly folded behind his back. He's never been one to show his emotions—he could be panicking or itching for a fight, but we'd never know. His brow furrows, and the way a muscle in his jaw clenches has me curling my hands into fists.

"Chaos," he says, opening his eyes. I don't miss the hint of excitement swirling in his eyes, but there is just as much concern, too. "Those closest to our ship...their minds are fractured, splintered by pain and panic. I can't make out exactly what happened."

"I can," Cari says. "My father." Her words are as cold as the ice I can see kissing her palms from where she stands next to me.

"Ready up," Talon says as he joins our group. He presses two black buttons situated between his thumbs and forefingers and his custom armor unfolds itself from the source, shaping to his muscles and protecting every inch of his body.

Tor's eyes crackle with lightning as the loading bridge slowly peels open.

Lock shifts into his shadow form, the midnight tendrils coiling at Cari's back.

The bridge barely touches the ground before Cari is racing down it with a stealth and speed that leaves the rest of us chasing after her. But she's quickly swallowed by the thick smoke, and I lose sight of not only her, but my brothers as we clear the landing. My boots crunch against the charred remains of grass, black soot floating around my ankles as I rush forward.

My eyes water, the smoke warm and nearly suffocating as I wade through it, latching onto that bond between myself and Cari, following it through the haze.

Cries ring out in the distance, the wails of the injured raking over my skin. I've heard those cries before, the anguished pleas for help after an attack. I run faster.

I skid to a halt once I'm clear of the thick layer of smoke, blinking the sting from my eyes as I scan the area before me.

The city is in ruins, only the homes and businesses carved straight into the base of the mountain still standing. All the little wooden homes that lined the dirt roads are consumed by hungry flames that are hopping from one house to the next, hissing and popping as they destroy everything in their path.

Younglings and their parents alike are trying to put out the flames, dumping buckets and bowls and even cups of water in an attempt to save their homes. But it's like throwing a grain of sand into an ocean of flame. Their jade-colored skin is covered in ash and soot and some are bleeding from injuries unknown.

A blink of time, that's all it takes for me survey the area and *move*.

Tor and Talon flank my left and right. Cari and Lock are nowhere to be seen.

"Tor," I call out to him as we run into the fray. "You take the left quadrant. Get the little ones out first and any survivors you can manage."

"On it," Tor says, rushing off.

"Talon," I continue. "Get in the air," I say, pointing to where the flames are growing above the city, threatening to raze its way up the mountains. "Find anything you can to stop the fire from spreading."

"Got it," Talon says, his suit of armor igniting like a sky ship as it propels him off the ground.

I race into the center of the city, where debris has fallen, trapping some of the Earth Realm citizens. Using all the strength I possess, I lift and toss fallen trees that are still burning, clearing a path for those pinned in. Terrified cries fill the air, along with the acrid scent of smoke.

Once I clear an area, I race to another.

And another.

But it doesn't matter how fast I move or how many people I save, that fire still rages.

I round the corner at the end of a main dirt road leading away from the residential area and find the source of the fire.

It's the Shattered Isle king's sky ship, and it's blazing, the flames nearly touching the sky as it reaches its fingers out, consuming everything it touches almost as if it has a mind of its own.

And standing right in the thick of it is my mate.

"Cari!" Her name is a strangled cry from my lips, my soul warring between seeing my mate in danger and needing to protect her, to shock and awe at the power she's wielding.

She doesn't even bother to turn or look my way, too focused on her work. On that ice and snow streaming from her palms as she battles the fire.

"Talon!" she yells, her head darting upward after she's gotten a section of the ship to stop burning. "I need to get in the air!"

Talon alters his path in the sky, spearing for her like a missile and picking her up just as quickly. They catapult into the sky, hovering right over the danger zone as the flames nearly lick their shoes.

But Cari...sun save us...she propels tons of ice and snow at the flames, suffocating the fire as Talon maneuvers her over the heart of it. The hiss of the dying flames gives way to more cries for help, and I snap into action. Home after home, business after business, I clear it, ushering the people out of the fire's path.

Shadows gather and slither in and out of buildings near me, catching flaming debris, or whisking younglings out of harm's way on an obsidian-colored wind.

*Lock.*

Shock ripples through my system as I continue to help as many as I can. Lock fighting on our side, helping without being ordered, is unfamiliar since we spent the last year chasing him down thinking he'd turned into a cold-blooded murderer. We'd been so painfully wrong about our estranged brother, and I'll spend the rest of whatever days I'm allowed to live making it up to him. Sure, he still walks that line between madness and clarity, he always has, but I will never doubt him again.

"Left quadrant is clear," Tor says once he's reached my side. Lightning curls around his arms, blazing in his eyes, and soot stains his cheeks.

"Right is too," Lock says, manifesting from his shadows on my other side.

"I've cleared the middle," I say, and we all look up to where Talon and Cari are still working to put out the last of the flames. I can feel the strain on my mate's power through our bond. "She's giving too much."

"I can feel it too," Tor grumbles. "Cari!" he calls up to the sky, chiding her with that one word alone. "Enough!"

She ignores him.

"Stubborn, darling," Lock mutters at my side, ever the picture of calm.

Panic spiderwebs from my chest as I can do nothing but watch as my mate empties her caches of power, draining herself to the dregs as she sends wave after wave of ice and snow over the last remaining flames. Her body goes limp in Talon's arms as she extinguishes the last of it, and I swear I can feel the threads of our bond strain as he flies her toward us.

"You should've stopped her," I snap at Talon, reaching for her.

"I tried," he says, handing her over to me and pressing the buttons on his hands, his armor retreating into contraptions so he can meet my eyes. "She wouldn't listen."

I glare at him as I gather my unconscious mate in my arms, knowing my anger is misplaced. I'm livid about the fire, about who started it, not at my brother for not being able to dissuade our dear wife from sacrificing her own well-being to save others.

Pride and panic mingle together, tightening my chest as I look down at her. Her cobalt skin is covered in dark soot, her hair is caked in it, and her eyes are closed. Her chest rises and falls easily, though, offering me some clarity to think.

The citizens of the Earth Realm are gathering around us, some looking awestruck while others look rageful. The energy around us shifts, a sensation in the atmosphere that has my spine straightening. I move toward Lock, handing Cari over to him.

"Get her back on the ship," I command, my tone low between us. While I've accepted my brother and know all he's done to save us, the public is still wary of him, and with the way they're looking at him and my queen? Getting them out of sight is the best for all of us.

Lock dips his head, shifting into shadows that curl around her body before whisking away.

Arms free, and mind clear now that I know she'll be safe and attended to, I turn to face the gathering crowd. There are more angry faces than relieved. Talon and Tor flank my left and right sides as we shift to face them.

"How do you want to play this?" Talon whispers the question at me.

And it's in that moment that I realize *we* are the kings of the All Plane, the rulers who are responsible for all the other realms, from the elemental and instrumental and all the others in between. Us. Our decision. Our mistakes to make or wounds to heal.

I'd been crowned several days ago after my father's death, but I hadn't truly felt it until this moment.

The weight of that truth settles heavy over my chest as I meet the accusing eyes of the Earth Realm people.

"That's your wife's father's ship!" a male spits, pointing his fingers at the ruined ship. "He did this!"

"Is he still here?" Tor interjects, ignoring the anger in the male's voice.

"He stole another ship," a female from the group says. Her voice is softer, yet there's still a great deal of distrust in her eyes. "Set that one on fire before he left."

"His guards wrecked our homes," another female says, tears rushing down her cheeks. "They took everything we had."

"My brother is dead because of him!" another male shouts, a bloody gash on his forehead. "The queen must answer for this!"

"Your queen almost killed herself to save you!" Talon fires back, his voice icy-hot and taking no prisoners. He and Tor look ready to battle every single one of them who speaks poorly of our mate, but I raise my hands before each of them, silently commanding them to back down.

I can't stand that kind of talk about our mate, either, but these people have just endured an unprovoked attack from an enemy they couldn't stand against. We have to be understanding of that. Which is why I cast an apologetic gaze across all their faces as I walk in the circle that has formed around us.

"I understand your anger," I say, loud enough for everyone to hear. "You didn't deserve this. Your realm is peaceful and the Shattered Isle king took advantage of that."

"What are you going to do?" a voice calls from the crowd. "News has spread. Your father is dead. Is this what we can expect from you and your brothers' rule?"

I swallow hard, shaking my head. "No," I say. "You can expect help. Aid. We will bring in All Plane troops to help you rebuild your beloved city. You will not be left in this alone—"

"We were alone and bleeding before you showed up!" someone snaps.

"We are officially at war with the Shattered Isle," I say.

"Your wife's home!"

"The Shattered Isle king's days are numbered, I promise you that," I continue. "My wife, your queen, stands with us, with the All Plane, and represents all the realms as we track the Shattered Isle king across the skies."

"How can we trust what you say is true?" a female asks, her eyes devastated, her fingers blistered from the flames. "You're married to a Shattered Isler." She waves those destroyed hands toward the wreckage all around us. "This is what they stand for. This is what they do, what they've always done. How can we believe a word you say when you're married to one? Who's to say she doesn't corrupt all your minds?"

The crowd grumbles their agreement with each question the female asks, the energy building and growing to riot levels.

Lightning streaks across the sky, thunder clouds rolling in and darkening the skies.

I glance over my shoulder at Tor and shake my head.

The thunder softens, but remains on alert.

"You can trust our history," I call out loud enough to quiet the crowd. I pace around the circle, meeting their eyes, imploring them with my own. "You can trust the relationships we've held for over two hundred years," I continue. "Our wife is from the Shattered Isle, yes," I say, nodding and grinding my teeth when a few of the people spit on the ground at the mention of her. "But her heart is true. She wants to join our peoples in the hopes of bringing peace between our realms."

Some of them scoff, some of them tilt their heads in intrigue.

"And if you can't trust me or my brother's words—the kings of the All Plane who have always answered your calls of need —then trust this. Cari is our *mate*—a true bonding that succeeds all other bonds. There is no us without her or her without us."

Some startled gasps roll through the crowd. True bonded mates are a rare thing among our kind, which makes Cari all the more rare and special in my eyes. She was made for us and us for her and it's time the realms understood that.

"The sun and stars would not match us if her intentions aligned with her father's," I continue. "He's the enemy. He's the one who is wreaking havoc across the skies right now because he didn't get what he wanted—all of us dead. And he'll keep not getting what he wants because we will not stop until his reign of terror is over. Once and for all."

Most of the crowd nods, agreeing with my promise.

I nod to the people who still look at me with distrust. "This is what he wants," I say. "He wants the realms in chaos, in disarray, separate and fighting each other. He wants us to war with each other while he makes his move to steal our throne. We can't give him what he wants. He has never earned anything in his life except for a death sentence." I blow out a breath. "Can you say the same of us? Can you stand there and forget the peace and love between our realms?"

"No," a female says from the crowd, and many nod their agreement. "We're with you," she says, bowing slightly.

The rest of the crowd follows suit, bowing before me and my brothers, but I can still see the undecidedness on some of their faces. Their wounds were struck deep today, and they won't soon forget it.

We'll just have to do whatever it takes to earn their trust again.

"We will call for aid," I finally say as the tension in the crowd settles. "For now, please come to me or my brothers with your needs, and we'll help each of you."

I glance back at Talon, who nods and heads toward the ship to call Storm. He'll order All Plane soldiers here and a gob of supplies. It will take time, but we won't leave them starving.

Lines form as people rush toward me and Tor, and I take a deep breath, centering myself to focus on their needs, and not think about the monster escaping farther and farther the longer we remain.

"Can I join you?" Cari's voice sounds from behind me, where I stand under the stream of the shower in my room on the ship, and I whirl around.

She stands with nothing but a white cotton towel around her body, her long legs bare and beautiful, her hair down and caked in soot.

"Always," I say, extending a hand toward her.

Shedding the towel and hanging it on a hook outside the glass shower doors, she steps into the steam, sliding her hand into mine.

I gently pull her toward me, and she steps underneath the steady stream of hot water, sighing at the contact.

"Are you in any pain?" I ask, gathering another handful of soap and lathering it before I slide my fingers into her hair.

She turns, her ass grazing against my hardening dick, and I shudder as I work her hair into a lather. "No," she says, leaning into my touch as I massage her scalp. "Drained, for certain. But it doesn't hurt."

I wash the soot from her hair, guiding her under the water to rinse before I soap up her back. Inch by inch, I glide my hands over her smooth skin, relishing the tiny gasps or whimpers she utters as I take my time.

"You scared me today," I admit, turning her to face me when I've gotten her all clean.

She looks up at me apologetically. "I know," she says, shaking her head. "I'm sorry, Steel," she continues. "Everything that my father does...it's my responsibility to stop it, to stop him."

I tip her chin up, forcing her to meet my gaze. "It's our responsibility," I correct her. "You are not in this alone."

A soft, broken smile shapes her lips as she smooths her hands over my chest. The touch is electric, and I slide my hand over her hip, drawing her closer. "You've been distant," she says. "The fight between you and Talon over Blaize? Is that what's causing it?"

I nod, unable to lie to her. "I'm not trying to distance myself from you," I assure her, teasing the length of her spine with my fingers. She arches into the touch, like a cat begging for more pets. "Blaize has been my most trusted friend for centuries," I admit. "But Talon can't see past the mistakes he's made…" I trail off, shaking my head. "He never saw eye to eye with my father or the way he ruled in most recent years. Blaize openly expressed it and challenged the king many times. Talon hates him for it, but now…"

"Now you know the truth of your father's betrayal," she says. "His plans. And it makes you wonder if Blaize simply saw it first."

I nod again, sliding my hand from her back over her shoulder, down the center of her chest, and palm her breast. She gasps as I roll and play with her nipple, and I lean down to suck the peaked bud into my mouth.

Her fingers grip my hair as I do the same to her other breast. "You're making it extremely hard to focus on the conversation, Steel," she says, her words breathy.

I grin, glancing up at her from where I lean down, sucking and flicking her nipples until they're peaked and flush for me. "Maybe that's my intention, wife," I say against her delicious breasts.

"But, Steel," she says, her breath hitching when I sink to my knees before her. "I'm here for you. I want you to be able to talk to me."

"I am talking to you," I say, maneuvering her until her spine kisses the wall, the stream of hot water cascading down her body. "And I love you," I continue, my hands gripping her delectable hips. "But when I saw you today, felt you drain your power to the dregs, it *terrified* me. All I want now is to feel you, to touch you and kiss you and know that you're okay, that you're here, safe, with me."

She visibly swallows as she looks down at me, her eyes churning with love and need. "I love you," she whispers the words. "And I'm not going anywhere."

"No," I say, every inch of my voice a command. "You aren't."

Cari gasps as I spread her legs apart and dip my head between her thighs, the water rolling off her and gliding over my back. I hook one leg over my shoulder, bracing it there while I keep her steady by holding her hips.

"Steel," she sighs my name as I flick my tongue out, her flavor bursting on my tongue and unleashing every inch of my mate instincts.

I slide my tongue from slit to clit, relishing the taste of her as I grip her hips, moving her to rock into me like I know she loves. Thrusting my tongue inside her heat, I savor every moan, every gasp as I wind her up, her thighs clenching each time I circle her clit with the tip of my tongue.

Her fingers grip my hair, and I cast a glance upward, need slamming into me at the sight of her head thrown back against the shower wall, her eyes closed and brow pinched with need, the water beading over her gorgeous body, sliding over every dip and curve I plan to worship next.

I keep her steady with one hand, guiding my other to the apex of her thighs, and slide two fingers into her heat. I pump them while I tease her clit, circling around the sweet spot without giving her the exact pressure I know she needs.

"Steel," she moans, rocking into me with more abandon, and I groan. The way she chases her pleasure, the way her body is so responsive to me has my dick so hard it aches.

"You want to come, wife?" I ask, my lips moving in feather-light touches over her clit while I work her with my fingers.

"Stars," she sighs. "*Yes.*"

"How bad do you need it, mate?" My head is spinning from the taste of her, from the sound of her moans in my ears, from the way our bond is pulling tight and buzzing with need.

"So. Fucking. Bad. *Steel.*" She stresses each word with another roll of her hips over my face, and I can't help but smile at the desperation in her voice.

"You know I'll always give you what you need," I say, and pump her relentlessly with my fingers while flattening my tongue over her clit, giving her the pressure she needs.

A cry rips from her lips, her fingers digging into my hair so tightly a bolt of pain and pleasure races down my spine. Her pussy flutters around my fingers, and I quickly withdraw them, instantly replacing them with my tongue, needing her to come on my mouth. I groan at the heady taste of her, the heat of her surrounding me as her entire body trembles as she shatters for me.

I work her down with long laps and sweet flicks, only slowing to a stop when she's breathless. I don't give her long before I'm standing before her, hefting her up and up until she locks her ankles around my back and I'm sliding into her slick heat before she can blink.

"Steel, you feel amazing," she says, her eyes at my level. They're all hazy and lust-filled and begging for more as I thrust into her again and again.

"You're the best thing I've ever felt," I say, slanting my mouth over hers as I drive into her.

Her nails dig into my back as she can do nothing but hold on as I claim her body, the water streaming around us both, making our bodies slick and hot in all the best ways. I glide in and out of her, teasing her oversensitive flesh until she's clenching her hips around me so hard it almost hurts.

"Let go," she demands, and I don't need her to tell me twice. She knows me so well, my mate. Knows what I need.

I unleash myself from the chains I use to hold my power back and slam into her with abandon.

"Stars," she moans. "Yes."

Harder, faster, her cries increase with each time I slam home. Our powers ripple along the bond, twisting and inter-weaving as she takes all of me and I consume all of her. She's strength and ice rolled into one, my perfect match in every way.

"Steel!"

I slant my mouth over hers, drinking in her moans as she clenches around my dick, her body trembling again as one orgasm leads to another, every time I hit that spot deep inside her, sending her spiraling again and again.

The steaming hot water hisses as snow bursts all around us, and I grin at my mate, who is so lost in me, lost in us, that her power slips this way. She's restored, strengthened by our joining, and it feeds every mate instinct I have to take care of her in this way.

"You're fucking incredible," I growl the words, palming her ass as I guide her body up and down on my dick, her muscles rippling with pleasure.

She kisses me then, submitting to me entirely I as wring every ounce of pleasure from her body she possesses, and the act has my own orgasm climbing up my spine. And when she sucks my tongue into her mouth, hungry and demanding, I spill into her, my vision darkening for a few seconds before stars dance across my eyes.

Slowly, I continue to rock inside her, working her through the throes of it until her body is limp and languid around mine. Her breathing slows, her eyes sleepy and filled with love as she meets my gaze.

"Come, wife," I say, and she laughs.

"I just did."

I grin at her, shutting off the water with my free hand before stepping out of the shower. "Let's get you dry, then get you into a warm bed."

I gently set her on her feet, grabbing the towel and wrapping it around her body. Before I can start drying her though, she reaches up, cupping my cheeks as she kisses me. The kiss is gentle, loving.

"You are the perfect male," she says, and there is a depth in her words that encompasses so many unspoken things.

I graze my finger over her cheek. "Only for my mate," I answer. Because it's the truth. I'm perfect for her because she's perfect for me. And the rest of the world can be damned, as long as she's at my side.

## 8
## CARI

*T*he smell of smoke lingers in the air, but the fresh snow atop the mountains is doing its best to combat it with a crisp, fresh scent. My mates and I only slept for an hour before returning to the city to help in any way we were capable—mostly clearing debris and wreckage and distributing what food we could spare from our own stores on the ship.

Storm has already dispatched four All Plane ships that should arrive before night's end, which helps soothe the anxiety clawing at my throat any time I stop for a moment to *think*. If I'm moving, I don't think about the fact that my father did this to a city of innocent people. If I keep helping cleanup, regardless of how exhausted I feel, I'm not thinking about how far away he's getting from us. How much sky he's putting between me and him.

A tiny gasp sounds from my right as I'm walking down the main city road after helping a block of businesses clean up their damaged shop and goods. I whirl toward the sound, eyes landing on a youngling no more than a quarter of the way into her life. Her brown hair hangs in messy curls around her jade face, but her brow is pinched as she looks down at her little leg, which is beneath a fallen beam from the building in which she sits.

I hustle through the broken windows, my boots crunching against the glass as I shift and plop into the store.

The youngling flinches when I crouch before her, examining her leg and the beam.

"It's all right," I say. "I'm Cari. I won't hurt you."

Terror shimmers in her eyes as she takes me in, no doubt the horrors of the evening prior playing out in her mind. Even if she doesn't know who I am, I'm undoubtedly a Shattered Isler, and after what my father's guards did to her people, I don't blame her for the reaction.

And part of me knows that's my father's intention—to ruin any chance I may have at bringing our two realms together, to finally have peace.

"What's your name?" I ask, running my hands along the large wooden beam where it sits over her leg, ensuring that when I move it, I won't further harm the youngling.

"Tris," she says, her bottom lip wobbling a little.

"You're very strong, Tris," I say, shifting in my crouch and situating my fingers beneath the beam. "This is extremely heavy and you're not even crying."

Pride beams in her eyes.

"You remind me of my best friend, Gessi," I say, wanting to distract her before I pry the beam up. "She's from your realm," I continue. "And she's the smartest, strongest person I know."

"She's from my realm?"

"Yes," I say. "But she's lived with me for as long as I can remember. More like a sister. Do you have any siblings?"

The little one shakes her head. "Just me and my pop," she says. "This is our store. I was trying to clean when this fell just now. He's visiting the kings to ask for assistance with our lost products."

I nod. "I'm sure they'll do their best to help," I say, then keep my eyes focused on hers. "You ready?" I ask.

She nods, clenching her little eyes shut as I heave the beam upward. My muscles quiver from the weight of it, but Tris manages to roll out from underneath it quickly. I set the beam down, kneeling before her once again.

Tears fill to the brim of her eyes as she sees her mangled leg.

"Do you have a healer here?" I ask her, and she nods. "May I?" I ask, extending my arms toward her.

"Su...sure," she says, tears rolling down her cheeks.

I scoop her up as gently as possible, cradling her tiny frame to my chest as I carefully tiptoe through the wreckage, the broken window, and finally make it back onto the main street. I follow her directions and do my best to ignore the accusing glares shot my way by the people we pass.

"I have a youngling here!" I call into the overcrowded tent that's been set up to treat the wounded.

A flurry of healers work over the large interior of the tent, but one hustles to my side, noting Tris's leg and ushering me to an empty cot to our right. I set her on the cot, and then the healer is shoving me aside with a disgruntled snort, dismissing me as if I were nothing but Shattered Isle trash.

Anger flares, sizzling in my chest as I part my lips—

"That's better, isn't it?" the healer asks Tris, the healing emerald light glittering onto her broken leg and mending the wound right before my eyes.

"Yes, thank you," Tris says, her little head falling back against the cot, eyes closing in exhaustion from the ordeal.

Anger is replaced with shame and regret. My fault. All my fault. If I'd just chased my father down and killed him before he got here, if I would've listened to my instincts instead of being convinced I needed to be crowned first to earn the realm's loyalty and trust, none of this would've happened.

None of this would've happened if my father wasn't the monster he is.

I swallow hard, backing out of the tent and running into a group of people with scowls on their faces. They form a horseshoe around me, fingers curling into fists at their side.

"I bet my life if we hand you over to your father he'll promise to never set foot inside our realm again," a male says, his hair acid-white with eyes that match.

I note the formation around me, the six males herding me away from the healer's tent. Smart. Wouldn't want any damage to occur there and risk their people's health. I allow them to back me onto a sidewalk, pressed up against a few wrecked buildings that reek of charred meat and ash.

"He might even pay us for the damages too," another one says.

"He has to have a bounty on his princess's head after she flipped sides—"

"You're all idiots if you think my father will ever give you anything you want," I snap, unable to quell the anger boiling in my blood.

"Bold of you to talk to us like that," the first male says. "When we have you cornered and your precious husbands are nowhere in sight."

He isn't wrong. Talon, Tor, Steel, and even Lock are all working endlessly to assist the citizens here and are scattered throughout the city.

"An even bigger fool to think I need my mates to protect me," I fire back.

They tighten their half-circle around me, and I raise one finger. "Ah-ah," I say, allowing a flicker of ice to burst from my fingertip.

Several of them flinch and draw back, but two are bold enough to remain where they are, their hands outstretched, a length of rope poised and ready for the trapping.

I take a deep breath through my nose, letting it out through my mouth, and graze my finger over the necklace I wear. CB-1 immediately flares to life, and I whisper for him to retrieve Lock. I can call for any of my mates, but Lock will be the most understanding if this encounter goes south.

"Fear makes people do terrible things sometimes," I say in the calmest voice I can muster as CB-1 flies away. "I understand your fear—"

"We're not scared of you, Isler," one male spits while the others are gaping at where CB-1 just flew past them.

"And yet, your actions scream otherwise," I say. "Only someone who feels like their back is against the wall would attempt to make a deal with the Shattered Isle king—"

"Your father."

"Yes," I say, searching for patience. These people have every right to hate me. I'm the princess of the evil king who just set their city on fire. I'm a direct line to their suffering, but didn't any one of them see me put out the flames? "He is my father. Which means I know him better than any of you ever will." I shake my head. "He will reward you if you turn me over to him by sliding a knife into each of your backs."

A few of the males visibly swallow, taking another step back.

"This isn't the answer," I implore to the two who remain in an attack position. "Violence isn't the answer. Fighting amongst ourselves won't help us stop who is really to blame —my father."

"And his people—"

"Wrong," I cut over the male who holds the rope. "You're wrong about my people," I say. "Some of them are like what you witnessed yesterday, that I can't deny, but not *all*. There are good, gentle, loving people in the Shattered Isle. People like you. Who are just trying to make it by, to feed their families, to take care of their loved ones. Those are the people I'm fighting for. Them and *you*."

The male lowers the rope, his eyes churning with curiosity.

"Dirk," he says, clutching the leader's shoulder. "You saw what she did yesterday. With the ice. She could've killed us by now."

Dirk glares at me, then glances back to his buddies, who are nodding their agreement.

"This was a bad idea," the rope male says. "We're just…"

"Angry," I answer for him. "You want a quick fix, an instant gratification for the blows they dealt you and your people. Trust me, I understand that sentiment very well."

Shadows gather to my right, but don't form into anything more than wisps.

"I'm not your enemy. My mates are not your enemy. We're here to right the wrongs delivered to you and to any of the other realms who may suffer the same fate." My heart clenches with the notion, but I press on. "We have one common enemy, and he is nowhere near here. That's where the fight is. And that's where I'll go."

The males part as I walk forward, leaving their plans to trap and ransom me to my father behind. CB-1 slides along my neck, settling back into his necklace form just as Lock materializes from the shadows.

"That was very queen-like of you, darling," he says, keeping pace with me as I walk away from the business district of the city.

"They wanted to ransom me," I say, shaking my head.

"You could've sliced their tongues from their mouths," Lock says, arching a brow at me as we walk. "Is that why you rang for me?" he smirks.

"I know how much you like a little chaos," I say, my soul lightening just a little at his jokes after the heavy morning.

"Especially when you're in the middle of it," he coos.

"How are things going on your end?" I ask as we near our ship.

"Well, no one tried to kidnap me and sell me to the Shattered Isle king, so I'd say a shade better than you."

I laugh, but it's quickly cut off by Steel.

"What?" he asks from where he stands near the ship, a group of people leaving his side from where they must've been asking him for help. Talon and Tor head over with him. "Someone tried to kidnap you?"

I wave him off, but lightning cracks the space between Tor and Talon.

"I'll fry them," Tor says, hand already curled in a fist.

Talon merely narrows his gaze at me, a cold sort of anger there at the mention of what happened.

"I handled it," I say, trying to assure them. I look at Steel, who reaches for me. "I promise. I'm fine. They're scared. That's all."

"She handled it very diplomatically," Lock says, arms folded behind his back. "You would've been proud, brother," he says to Talon, who still hasn't spoken.

Steel opens his mouth, but CB-1 buzzes against my neck, stopping him. I hurry to slide my finger along the blue stone, and the little robot manifests before me, illuminating Gessi in midair.

"Gessi," I say, relieved to see my friend. I haven't dared try to contact her, knowing her position in General Payne's life.

"I don't have much time," she says, and I immediately sense the panic in her voice.

"Are you discovered?" I ask, stepping closer to the holographic image of her. "Are you hurt?"

"No," she says. "But I overheard the general talking about a planned attack on the Fire Realm," she says, voice hushed and hurried. "I also heard him saying something like thirty percent of the Corters have pledged their allegiance to your father. I don't know if he's there or heading that way, but Cari...not everyone in the Fire Realm will side with him. And you know what they'll to do those people who refuse to join."

"All too well," I say, heart racing. The Earth Realm is evidence enough of what my father is capable of when he doesn't get his way. He's done sitting on the Isle, waiting for his moment. He's taking his failed plans with the All Plane king out on anyone and everyone he can.

"When is the attack?" I ask.

"Tomorrow," she says, and I gasp. "I have to go." She flashes me a broken smile, then disappears.

CB-1 waits for my instruction, blinking that little blue eye at me before I nod and slide my finger over him. He wraps himself around my neck, the robotic jewelry becoming almost a comfort now.

"We'll have to leave immediately," Steel says.

All my mates remained quiet and calm during the message, but I can see their eyes churning now, plotting, strategizing.

"If we fly fast enough, we might make it in time," Tor says.

Steel nods. "Alert the people," he says to Tor. "Storm's soldiers should be here within the next few hours. They won't be unguarded for long."

Tor nods and races away.

Talon is already spinning on his heels, bounding up and into the ship to ready it for takeoff.

I'm frozen. Even as Steel follows Talon, I can't move. Can't think or breathe or see around the images playing out in my mind.

The Fire Realm, the innocents there screaming and crying out for help that just isn't there. The good people trying to fight against a threat they're not even remotely trained to protect themselves against.

And my father, at the head of it, laughing manically at the blood he sheds—

"Darling," Lock whispers, his hand sliding along my back.

I blink out of the horrific images in my mind, grounding myself in the present by concentrating on my mate's touch, his voice calling to me.

"It may not be like that," he says, his blue-green eyes all too knowing. "We may yet make it."

"In my head, mate?" I accuse, but there is no anger there. I've always allowed him past my mental barriers when so many have fought their entire lives to keep him out.

"Should I not be?" he asks, drawing me closer. "Would you rather weather that storm alone?"

I press my lips together and shake my head.

The ship whirs to life next to us, and Tor returns, arching a brow at the pair of us, holding each other like we're not in a hurry to go to another battle.

"There's time for that later," Tor chides, anticipation flaring in his eyes. "To the skies. Blood awaits!"

I huff out a laugh as he races into the ship, then glance up to Lock. He doesn't have to say anything. I can feel his support wrapping around the bond, and his thirst for revenge matches mine. We board the ship, silent as Talon propels us into the skies, and all I can do is sit there and *hope*.

Hope that we're fast enough.

Hope that we catch my father.

And hope that I'm enough to kill him.

* * *

Over two dozen Shattered Isle guards tear their way through the pubs that offered us meals and shelter not two weeks ago.

Corters lay slaughtered and bleeding in the streets. Rain comes down in sheets, causing rivers of red to trace their way down the cobblestone paths.

Screams crack the air, along with the sound of swords splitting flesh.

The fighting is everywhere at once—some Corters are on the side of the Shattered Islers, battling their ilk as they try to make everyone in the city bend to them.

My mates and I barely landed before we raced into the battle, but we're severely outnumbered.

With some of the Corters siding with my father's guards, there's barely a chance to breathe between dispatching one enemy to the next.

My skin is slick with my own blood and the blood of those I've taken out.

I race from group to group, my ice daggers finding homes in the hearts of those who are trying to slaughter the innocents —the females and younglings and elderly who have no way of defending themselves.

"More incoming!" Steel shouts from across the street where he battles three Corters who are using their razor-sharp horns atop their head against him. He knocks one across the road with his sheer strength, then points up.

A Shattered Isle ship bearing General Payne's grotesque emblem—a severed head with a snake coiling from an eye-socket—bears down in the center of the city, landing atop a roof of a brick building that shudders from the ship's weight.

The doors open, and twenty Shattered Isle soldiers leap out, surrounding Steel in an instant.

My heart leaps to my throat, everything around me slowing down like it's coated in a thick sap.

I'm screaming for him while fighting off the four Corters trying to get through me.

Lock's shadow is too far to call for.

Talon is fighting on the roof of a building blocks away.

Tor is lighting up the skies and raining lightning down on everything he can behind me.

Steel is alone.

He's outnumbered.

And yet, he tips his chin, defiant as ever, and raises his fists as the Shattered Isler soldiers converge around him, laughing and sneering.

I slice through the Corter in front of me, moving in Steel's direction only to be slammed back by two more Corters. Their hits feel like being run over by a sky ship, and it steals the breath from my lungs.

The Shattered Isle soldiers move, swords drawn on my mate, and I'm shaking so hard ice and snow blast from me in every direction, slicing through the Corters around me and almost taking out a few innocents along the way. Luckily, they're hunkered down in the buildings behind me.

"Steel!" I yell as I move to race to him, only to be hauled back by another Corter, his meaty claws around my ankle. My chest smacks against the slick cobblestones, the breath heaving from my lungs and my teeth rattling in my skull.

I whirl around, swiping my free leg across the Corter's face, knocking him clean out before scrambling to my feet.

The blade of the closet Shattered Isle solider is at Steel's throat.

I'm too far away.

My legs are useless hunks of rubber as I try to run to him—

The ground trembles as something slams in front of Steel, the force of the blow sending the soldiers flying backward, some of their swords clipping each other as they hit the ground.

I skid to a halt when I reach Steel's side.

"Blaize?" Steel says, his chest heaving.

Blaize smirks at Steel over his shoulder, flexing the muscles in his arms as he raises his fists toward the gathering soldiers who are getting to their feet. Blaize shrugs. "You didn't think I'd let you have all the fun, did you?"

Steel just shakes his head, lining his shoulder up with Blaize's, me on the other side to form a triangle, spinning to focus on the surrounding soldiers.

"Couldn't be away from me for a second, could you?" Steel teases.

"You know how boring life is without you," Blaize says.

I choke out a broken laugh. "Remind me to thank you when this is over," I say before all the relief and levity disappear.

Because the soldiers are back on their feet, blades drawn as they rush for us.

# 9

# TOR

*W*e're outnumbered. The streets are covered in blood and the innocents are hiding, hoping we can offer them a reprieve soon.

Steel, Cari, and Blaize are ahead, relentlessly fighting the Shattered Isle soldiers and Corters. I was trying to make my way to Steel when he'd been surrounded, but the Corters were dying left and right, and I couldn't leave them defenseless. Thank the sun Blaize showed. I may not like the bastard, but his timing is impeccable.

To my right, a Shattered Isle guard bears down on a Corter defending his tavern. He misses a sword swing by mere inches, then rams his horn-covered head into a Shattered Isle guard's stomach, the squelching sound of tearing flesh reaching across the cobblestone pavement to where four Shattered Ilsers sprint toward me.

"Nicely done!" I yell to the Corter, winding up my arm as I gather my lightning, drawing all the power to gather in one giant ball I send hurtling straight for the approaching enemies.

Electricity cracks through the air, hitting each target. They're blown off their feet and flung backward. They don't get up again.

Blood pumps through my veins, hot and filled with adrenaline. Everything inside me narrows to the battle, to the feel of my power spiraling around my arms.

A crunch sounds behind me, and I whirl around, dropping to my knees, a blade already in my hand. I swipe faster than the enemy Corter can defend, slicing through his Achilles. He roars, his spine hitting the cobblestones as he reaches for his sword. My dagger finds a home in his heart, and he falls silent.

Something hard hits my back, and I turn to face my opponent, striking a bolt of lightning at his hammer-like weapon. It clatters to the ground, but the Corter keeps coming, rushing me with two Shattered Islers flanking him. I draw three large bolts, stopping them in their tracks.

Over and over again.

Blood and sweat and lightning.

I finally manage to clear the small section of defenseless businesses, nodding to the Corter who'd defended his tavern bravely.

It's strange to be fighting *for* the Corters, as we've had a tentative peace between us for the past decade. And since the last time we were here, one of them tried to assassinate Talon, but managed to harm Cari instead, this is the last place I thought I'd be defending. But the Shattered Isle king attacked, and we can't damn the innocents here because of a few radicals.

The cobblestones are slick with blood as I leave the newly cleared area behind, heading toward the center of the Corteran city.

Cari is fighting a Shattered Isler, but even as her ice daggers clang against his sword, her eyes are darting all over the area. She's looking for her father. Waiting for him to show himself, but he's a coward. He'll sacrifice all his men to get away. She meets my gaze as she slams an ice dagger into the Isler's throat.

"Tor, behind you!"

A loud snap sounds behind me, and I spin around. An Isler has a knife raised, but his eyes are lifeless and his neck is twisted at an odd angle. His knees crack against the pavement at my feet.

"Watch your back, Tor," Blaize says, glancing down at the dead enemy for a moment before he rushes back to Steel's side. Together, they fight off another group trying to destroy as many buildings as they can, and the innocents inside.

I span the distance between Cari and myself, skidding to a stop before her. I gently grip her chin in my fingers, examining the cut above her eyebrow. Every instinct is roaring at me to slaughter the one who put that wound there, but I know she already has.

Lock's shadows gather at my side, then he materializes out of them. "My section is clear," he says with an almost feline grin.

There isn't a speck of blood or grime on him, and it sends ice down my spine to think of how he dispatched an entire quadrant of enemies without even getting a little blood on him. It's unnatural, but fuck me, I'm glad he's on our side.

"You need help," he says, eying Cari.

I cast a concerned glance at her, too. "You're draining yourself again, little wife."

Cari is exceptionally strong, but she has an issue with tempering her power. She seems content to blow through her stores of it with no regard for her own safety.

"Darling," Lock chides, curling a shadow down her shoulder.

"I'm fine," she says, eying both of us.

I eye her right back, but drop it. We don't have time for arguments right now.

"Talon is going to lose his shit when he sees Blaize is here." I nod to where he fights next to Steel.

"Excellent," Lock says, his grin deepening as he scans the area. "Where is Talon?"

I look to the skies. No doubt he's stopping attacks from above, but before I can answer, more soldiers round a corner, heading straight for Steel and Blaize.

Cari, Lock, and I race over to them, creating a circle as the remaining Shattered Islers and enemy Corters surround us.

"Wife, are you ready?" I ask.

"I've got this. Let's end this and find my father!"

An ice blades forms from her palm as she runs towards the approaching soldiers.

Fuck, I love her.

We rush behind her, taking out the stragglers she leaves standing.

Shattered Islers stiffen before they can even reach Lock, their eyes wide and mouths gaping at whatever he makes them see. They fall shortly after, as if their hearts stop dead from fear.

Blaize and Steel work together as an effortless unit, using their enhanced combat skills to leave none standing. And I bring down lightning in waves.

But even with all that, these bastards keep on coming.

The ground shakes beneath my boots, and I hear our sky ship approaching. Talon unleashes a blaze of fire onto our enemies, wiping them all out as we finally catch our breath. He lands the ship in the wide open street behind us.

"You're welcome," Talon yells as the loading bridge opens us.

"We had them," I grumble, but I'm honestly happy for the break.

Talon's fiery gaze is on Blaize, ignoring my jab altogether.

Cari quickly runs to Talon while Steel looks over to his friend.

"Any sign of my father?" she asks Talon, who breaks his silent stare-down with Blaize, and shakes his head.

Cari gazes over the wreckage, over the distraught faces of the innocent Corters who were the target of this attack.

"Anyone who refuses to bend to him suffer if he isn't stopped," Cari says, exhaustion lining her features.

"He sacrificed his men to escape," Steel says.

"We need to figure out where he went before more cities are attacked," Cari says, pacing before the loading bridge, her eyes distant as if she's trying to calculate the king's next move. She, like Talon, will continue to blame herself for her father's choices.

"We will," Steel assures her. "Unlike your father, we have more allies. And we have each other." He wipes away the blood on her face.

The Corters who remained by our side are gathering behind us, weary but breathing.

"Do you expect King Jerrick to return?" asks the larger male who defended his tavern.

"He's on the move again," Steel says. "I don't anticipate him returning, but if he does, you can be assured *we* will return." Steel, ever the perfect diplomat, goes on to ensure them he'll call for more aid from the All Plane to help with the aftermath of the battle.

"My brothers and I will remember this!" I say enthusiastically as we board the ship.

The Corters nod, following Steel's instructions to pick a central location for the relief efforts, and gather amongst themselves at the still-intact tavern across the street. They've lost brothers to King Jerrick, some of them have joined him while others were lost defending their homes, their businesses.

My blood reignites with the injustice of it all, and I can taste lightning on my tongue. And with the battle over, there is only one other outlet of release I need right now. I snap my gaze across the ship to my mate, and her eyes meet mine, understanding churning there.

"You're with me, little wife," I demand, curling my finger at her to follow.

She hurries to my side, and I grab her hand, tugging her as I head toward my designated room on the ship.

My body is still pulsing with energy from the battle, and I can feel Cari's adrenaline shivering down our bond, too.

"Before bath or after?" I ask.

"What?" Cari asks.

"You have two choices. I can fuck you now, blood and grime and all, or we can get clean first."

Her eyes flare at my declaration.

"Quickly," I say. "Or I'll choose for you."

"Bath," she hurries to say. "A fast one."

I smirk at her, loving that her need is matching mine. Even as I fill my tub with steaming hot water, she paces the length of the bathing chamber, her nervous energy practically crackling in the air.

We're both covered in blood—some of our own, but most from our enemies. I turn to face Cari and shed my battle-worn gear, grinning at her when she hurries to do the same. I step into the hot water, watching as she follows me in, her glorious body on display as she sits across from me. Silently, we wash in hurried movements, the anticipation stretching between us like a tightrope. Once I'm free of blood and grime, I lean back, soaking my sore muscles, content to watch her in the water as she finishes up.

Clean, she slides next to me, water sloshing over the lip of the tub as she reaches for me beneath the water, and wraps her pretty fingers around my hard cock.

"Cari," I say, sighing as I lean my head back, submitting to her stroking.

"You questioned me out there," she says, her voice breathy as she works her other hand to cup my balls.

I lift my head, cocking a brow at her. "Was I wrong?" I challenge, then hiss as she ups her pace, her grip tightening around my dick. The hot water makes her hands slick, and heat zaps up my spine.

"I didn't say that," she says and leans so close her pebbled nipples tease my chest. "But what would you do if I questioned you mid-battle?" Her lips meet mine, the tip of her tongue teasing mine before she pulls back.

I grip her hips, a low growl rumbling in my chest. "I would've kept battling," I admit, and victory flashes in her eyes, her stroking relentless.

I lift her effortlessly, and she loses her grip on my cock as I settle her on top of me, but don't sink inside her yet. I want to enjoy this.

I trail my hand down her breasts, over her stomach, before slipping into the apex of her thighs. She's slick from the water, and swollen with need. Sliding two fingers inside her, I rub her clit with my thumb, my free hand massaging her breast.

She arches into my touch, riding my hand as she chases her release. And once I feel her clenching, I pull my fingers away, and I swear ice crystalizes over the edges of our bath.

"You're coming on my cock tonight, little wife," I say, capturing her mouth in a kiss.

She whimpers, kissing me back with a hunger that radiates down our bond.

Gripping her hips, I stand, lifting us both out of the tub, and don't even bother to dry us off as I move us to my bed. We're all tongues and teeth as I lower her to the bed, my hands exploring every inch of her glorious body.

But the need in us both is stretching that bond tight, the adrenaline from the battle urging me to go faster.

I push on her knees, widening them enough to where I can see that glistening pussy of hers. Sun damn me, she's slick and swollen and ready for me.

Lightning crackles on my fingertips as I tease her nipples, just enough electricity to have her writhing beneath me. I grin as I kiss my way from her lips, down her neck, and linger on the peaked buds of her nipples. Her fingers rake through my hair, her breaths coming in ragged gasps.

"Tor," she pleads, but I'm too lost in the sweet, heady scent of her need to give into her so quickly.

I work my way down, flicking my tongue over her clit before going lower. I slide my hands beneath her ass, lifting her so I can lick her slit.

"Tor!" she gasps when I go lower, teasing that forbidden spot with my tongue before working my way back up, plunging my tongue into her pussy, fucking her like I plan to do with my cock soon. "Yes," she moans, fingers tightening in my hair as I continue to lap and suck and devour her. With her ass in my hands, all she can do is hold on while I unleash my mouth on her. "Oh, stars," she whispers as her thighs tighten around my cheeks, her body trembling as her flavor bursts on my tongue.

I lick her through the throes of her orgasm before lowering her back to the bed, but barely give her a second to breathe before I'm lining up my aching cock at her slick entrance. She looks up at me with hazy eyes, and I thrust inside, hard and fast, just like she likes, just like we both need.

She pulls me closer, claiming my mouth as her nails dig into my back hard enough to draw blood.

"Fuck, Cari," I growl, loving the mixture of pleasure and pain as I sink inside her over and over again. I pound into her, each thrust harder than the next, driven by the delightful moans spilling from her lips. I slip my arm beneath her lower back, hauling her hips up again so I can fuck her from a deeper angle.

Each time I hit that sweet spot inside her, she shivers and tightens around me. She's so fucking responsive, and I can't get enough. The bond between us flares and sparks, lightning crackling across the room as my own release climbs.

"Tor. Harder. *Please*," she begs, her pussy clamping around my cock, all searing silk.

"Fuck," I groan, slamming into her with abandon, ensuring each time I sink to the hilt, my pelvis grinds against her clit, giving her everything she needs to come.

"Yes, Tor!" Her nails dig into my back as her orgasm rips through her, taking me right along with her.

We collapse back to the bed, me keeping my weight braced on my arms so I don't crush her. I slant my mouth over hers, gliding my tongue along the edges of her teeth as I tease and work her down.

She cups my cheeks in her hands, breaking our kiss just long enough to look at me.

I grin, reading the look in her eyes well enough. "Again, little wife?"

She nods.

I trail my nose along hers before kissing her jawline. "Where now?"

"Against the wall," she demands.

I obey.

## 10

## CARI

"*H*e wasn't here," I say, shaking my head at the holographic image of Gessi.

It's been a few hours since Tor and I parted ways—him to check in with his brothers, and me to make contact with Gessi.

Her brow furrows. "You must've just missed him," she says, biting her bottom lip. Her tell for deep thought. She blinks a few times, determined as she focuses on me. "General Payne said it. Sent troops there. Why would he do that if not to aid your father?"

I blow out a breath, flashes of the battle playing on repeat in my mind. The blood, the damaged city, the heartless slaughter of unarmed Corters.

"I don't know," I finally say, and my stomach sinks. "After what happened in the Earth Realm and now the Fire Realm, I feel like I'm always one step behind him."

*"Again," father's voice rings out across the training ring.*

*My knees wobble as I try to force myself to stand, but they give out and I fall to the floor again. I've been training for hours and I can't remember the last time I've eaten or had a drink of water. I know voicing as much will only land me more hours in this star-forsaken-room.*

*I blow out a breath. At least I'm fighting against opponents my own age today. Yesterday it was a selection of father's newest recruits three times my age.*

*Today, it's the young males father and the general are raising to be known Shattered Isle assassins. They'll get to go on special assignments and wear the Shattered Isle emblems proudly as they do it.*

*Not me.*

*Never me.*

*No one will ever be allowed to know the Shattered Isle princess is truly an assassin. Even the guards and these young males think my training is only so I can protect myself if the evil All Plane princes and their king ever decide to invade our lands again.*

*Anger sizzles through my blood at the thought of the vile creatures who killed my mother. Who almost killed my father. The same royalty that declared our island separate from the other realms.*

*"Get. Up." Varian hisses at me.*

*The youngling is only one year ahead of me, but he's much taller and already his body is shaping with the muscles of what I'm sure will make an intimidating male when he comes of age. As of right now, he's just a big pain in my ass.*

*"You know the punishment," Crane says from behind me. Another one of father's Shattered Isle youngling selection. It's an honor upon the families to have a youngling selected for assassin training. Father compensates families well for taking their children. After*

*all, once you're selected, you never see your family again. Every-thing is about the mission, the training, and becoming a weapon, even in sleep.* "Come on, Cari," *he whispers, a plea in his voice.*

*He's the nicer of the two. He pulls his punches even when he knows he shouldn't, and he allows me to land blows of my own, even though he has the ability to see them coming a mile away.*

*"Maybe you want to fail," Varian whispers, stomping over to me. "Too hard for you, princess?" he asks, crouching down to meet my gaze. His teal eyes are searing, an emotion there I can't read as he slaps his palms against the floor.*

*I jolt backward, noting the way his hands shift into the obsidian claws and slick substance that can transform his entire body into a nearly unstoppable force if he wills it.*

*A shudder shakes my body at the memory—he's only fully shifted into the beast once before, at my father's demand. The sight of him, fully transformed into a creature of midnight and muscle and razor-sharp teeth with the ability to leap buildings or run as fast as a jungle cat, will forever be burned into my memory. No wonder my father demanded his service in the assassin program. Father loves power, covets it.*

*"Do you need me to encourage you, daughter?" Father calls from his throne on the dais where he watches.*

*Ice fills my blood, streaking from my fingertips and lashing out at the shifted hands of Varian.*

*Varian leaps backward, releasing his hold on the shift, a laugh on his lips as I get to my feet and face him.*

*He doesn't need to shift to beat me. He's faster, stronger, and has two years of training on me. Same as Crane, who flanks Varian's right side as they look at me, fists raised.*

*"No, father," I grind out the words, curling my hands into fists, the sound of ice cracking as I raise them. "Again," I say, nodding to the two.*

*Crane flinches, but nods.*

*Varian smirks at me, and I swear there's pride in his gaze—*

"Cari," Gessi says, her voice imploring as I shoot back to the present. The memory of the ruthless training I'd been raised on shakes loose like snow from a tree.

"I'm sorry," I say, pinching my brow.

"It's all right," she says, her voice soothing. If we were truly in the same room, she would've already made us some of our favorite hot tea, and we'd be sitting on my bed, doing anything and everything to make each other laugh. "I'll try to intercept the information faster next time," she says, eyes apologetic. "I didn't have an excuse to leave so quickly after I heard the information last time. I'll do better. I'll make something up, get the information to you faster—"

"Don't," I say. "You can't risk yourself any more than you already are. Besides, if you hadn't warned us, there would've been many more deaths. Despite the tentative relationship between the All Plane and the Fire Realm, there are innocent Corters here that were saved because of your information, Gessi. Be proud of that."

She sighs, but nods, her bunched shoulders relaxing a little from where ever she sits in the palace.

"Are you in your rooms?" I ask, wanting to change the subject, wanting to draw out our conversation a little longer.

"New rooms," she explains. "Closer to General Payne's in case he needs me in the middle of the day."

I gasp, revulsion rippling through me. "He's not forcing you to—"

"Stars, no," she says, a sliver of fear creeping into her tone. "At least, not yet. There have been looks..." She shudders, and I mimic her reaction. The general is three times our age, with a putrid disposition that matches his black heart. "He's assigned the bird to my door, though."

"Crane?" I ask, relief uncoiling some of the tension in my muscles. Shattered Isle assassin he may be, but *nothing* gets by him.

"Yes," she says, something fluttering over her features I can't make out. "Night and day," she says. "He's assigned to my side. You can imagine the chatter."

I laugh, and she joins in. Crane is silent on the best of days, hidden on more of them. You never know he's around until he wants you to know, and by that point—if you're an enemy —it's already too late.

"You're close," she says after a moment of silence bubbles between us.

I nod. "Not long now."

"He has to be coming back here, though I haven't heard the general say specifically."

"I wouldn't expect him to go anywhere else. He's rapidly losing soldiers. He'll need the protection of his palace and his assassins if he stands a chance against us." I tilt my head at that thought. "Is Varian assigned to you, too?"

She shakes her head. "He's been on a mission for weeks now," she explains. "I have no idea what General Payne ordered him to do, but it was at the start of his taking over rule on the Isle."

A shiver skates down my spine at the idea of Varian on the loose somewhere. We'd grown up together, and he'd always pushed me to be better in our training sessions, but he was the most ruthless of my father's elite assassins. He's the absolute last person I'd want to fight in this upcoming war, and I hated that I didn't have a clue if he'd stand with me or against me.

"Cari," Talon calls from my opened door. "We need you."

I nod at Talon, then look at Gessi. "We'll talk soon."

"I'll let you know the minute I hear anything."

My heart aches as we wave our hands in front of our CBs, the image of my best friend disappearing like a phantom wind. CB-1 floats to my side, his whirring a comfort as he lingers near my shoulder.

I turn to Talon, who's still staring at that vacant spot right where Gessi's holograph had been.

"What is it?" I ask, pushing off the bed and stopping before him.

He blinks a few times, then motions his head for me to follow him.

He leads me into the gathering area, where Tor, Steel, and Lock sit around a round metal table, all wearing near-identical looks of strain. I note that Blaize is nowhere to be seen, and half wonder if Talon threw him off the ship while I was speaking with Gessi.

"What's happened?" I ask, panic lashing through my body. "Has there been another attack?"

Steel scoots over on the bench where he sits, patting the spot beside him. I sink into the spot, our thighs brushing beneath the table. Talon claims the seat on the other side, while each of my husbands looks at me.

"Tell me," I demand, heart racing in my chest.

"River called," Tor says, his muscled forearms resting on the table, lightning crackling between his fingers as he wrings his hands.

"And?"

"There have been attacks at opposite ends of the borders of the All Plane," he explains.

"By who?"

"They're not sure," Steel answers.

"Then how do they know there were attacks?" I ask, confused.

"Whoever is doing it left a string of bodies behind," Lock says, his voice cool, calm.

I look between them, focusing on Tor. "Your soldiers?"

Tor gives me a curt nod, and I watch as his throat bobs. He's not one to show emotion openly, but I can feel the loss of his soldiers flickering down our bond. I send a burst of comfort toward him, silently promising they'll be avenged.

"Whoever it is, they're formidable," Steel continues. "They are expertly trained. Even Storm couldn't find tracks to follow. Almost as if they didn't need to set foot on the soil before killing them."

Everything inside me goes cold and still.

"My father?" I whisper the question, eyes darting to each of my mates. "You think it's somehow my father?" Acid crawls up my throat and my hands tremble where I grip them beneath the table.

Steel reaches across my thigh, separating my hands and interlocking his fingers in my own. He doesn't flinch at the ice pooling there that I can't control right now, doesn't jerk away. He takes the pain, all to ground me from the rising panic.

"You think he doubled back," I say, not asking this time.

Talon leans back in his seat, arms folded over his chest.

"But Gessi," I hurry to say. "She said he was headed here. And it makes sense. This is on the way home—on the way to the Shattered Isle. He needs that protection…" My voice trails off as another plan reveals itself like a flower blooming in the night. "Unless…"

"Unless he's using the rumors and assumptions about his whereabouts to thin out the protection around the All Plane," Steel finishes for me.

"He's right," Tor adds. "We've already dispatched a great deal of our armies to aid both the Earth Realm and the Fire Realm." He sighs. "There are six ships on their way here now to help after the battle."

"Gessi's information suggests otherwise," Lock says, and I nod.

"Either Gessi is lying," Talon says, finally speaking up.

"She wouldn't," I interrupt him.

"Or," he continues. "Maybe they're onto her secretly communicating with you."

Ice splinters around my heart at the thought.

"We don't know that, brother," Lock says. "They could plant false information throughout each of their units in order to throw off any hearsay that might occur. That's a common strategy for any general in any war."

Tor nods, but there's a wariness in his eyes as he looks to me, then Steel.

I glance between them and note the regret and longing in their eyes.

"No," I say, my heart clenching. "You're leaving?"

I can feel the instant battle down the bond from both of them just as well as I can feel the resolve in the notion that they have to go.

"Even if your father isn't there," Tor says, leaning over the table to reach for me. I give him my free hand, my other still in Steel's. "There is an assassin in the midst. He's testing our borders and putting everyone on high alert. Steel and River are fully capable, but…"

"Without their kings present, what will the people think?" I finish for him, and he nods.

"We don't want to leave you," Steel says, squeezing my hand. "But Talon and Lock agree. Tor and I must return to the All Plane while you three finish what you started. If you reach the Shattered Isle and he's not there, then you'll know where to go."

"And besides, little wife," Tor says, lightning sparking in his eyes. "You should be the one to end General Payne and free your people from the suffering he's causing."

I swallow hard, shoving down my selfish desires to have my mates by my side, and nod at him. "I won't lie to you," I say. "I hate the idea of not being able to protect you."

Tor laughs, a delightful booming sound that sends warm shivers down my spine.

Steel grins at me, smoothing his thumb over the back of my hand.

"How do you think we feel about you?" Steel offers, and I nod.

Lock offers us all a broken smile, then moves away from the table, shadows already curling around his back. He looks down at Talon. "Brother," he says. "Shall we go plot the demise of one Shattered Isle general?"

Talon blinks of out his thoughts, then nods as he follows Lock out of the room, no doubt giving me privacy with Steel and Tor before they leave. I swear, I love them all the more for it.

Talon and Lock are barely out of sight before Steel tugs me toward him, slanting his mouth over mine, consuming me with a frenzied kiss. He jerks back, tugging his shirt over his head, his sky-blue eyes churning with love and desire and unfiltered *need.* He unbuckles his pants and gets rid of them in a hurry, his already hard cock springing free.

My heart races, lava shooting through my veins as Steel slowly lifts me up, turning me to sit on his lap with my spine pressed against his bare chest. He plunges a hand down my top, palming my breast as he plants kisses along my neck and behind the shell of my ear.

Tor rounds the table with a predator's gaze before he drops to his knees before me. Hooking his fingers into the band of my cotton pants, he yanks them down my legs and tosses them behind him.

Steel shifts beneath me, his hard length teasing me from behind as he grips my thighs and spreads me wide before Tor.

Tor flashes me a delighted gaze before he sinks his head between my thighs. He slides his tongue straight through the heat of me, and I arch, my ass rubbing against Steel's hard cock as Tor laps at me from the front.

"Make our mate come," Steel demands, and the words clang through me, igniting every nerve ending I possess. He continues to hold my thighs apart, giving Tor all the access he needs to devour me.

My breaths are ragged as Tor fucks me with his tongue, alternating between thrusting inside and sucking my clit in his mouth until I can barely see straight.

I throw my head back against Steel's shoulder, giving him more access to my neck, which he teases with his mouth and teeth. I turn my head, and Steel is there, kissing me, drinking in my pleasured cries as Tor relentlessly pushes me toward that sweet, sharp edge.

My thighs tremble, the need to draw away from the intensity of Tor's tongue and mouth is overwhelming, but Steel holds me open, drawing out that intensity in a way that makes my head spin.

Tor draws back, shifting so he can slide two fingers into my aching heat. I rock into his hand, seeking out more, more, more. The motion has me grinding my ass on Steel's cock, and he groans, his fingers gently biting into my thighs.

Everything in me narrows to the feel of Tor's fingers inside me, his tongue working my clit in teasing circles that have me shaking with need. To the way Steel feels behind me, hard and strong and hot.

"That's it, little wife," Tor says as he pumps me, curling his fingers against that spot deep inside me. He looks up at me before he sucks my clit into his mouth, and I bow in Steel's lap as I shatter into a thousand pieces around Tor's fingers and mouth.

My body trembles as tendrils of electricity spark and skitter all over my body, relief unraveling me until I'm limp atop Steel's lap.

Tor grins at me as he unbuckles his belt and drops his pants, baring himself to me, but glances back at Steel. "Put her on her knees," he demands.

He may as well have sent one of his bolts of lightning down the center of me because heat zaps down my spine, my eyes widening—

Steel moves so fast I barely register it. One second I'm on his lap, the next I'm on all fours, one palm on either side of Tor's hips where he leans back on the floor. Tor fists his beautiful hard cock as I hover over him, Steel nudging my legs apart with his knee, lining himself up with my slick pussy.

Steel grazes his hands over my spine, around to my breasts, and down between the apex of my thighs, feeling the results of what Tor did to my body. Every stroke has me sparking with need, my body awakening again as the bonds between us curl and tighten.

I gasp as Steel teases me with the head of his cock, sliding in an inch, only to withdraw and roll his fingers over my clit instead. My fingers curl against the cool floor, my eyes hooded as I endure his teasing and watch Tor stroking himself.

Steel bends himself over me, kissing down my spine, over the globes of my ass, and back up before he reaches my ear. His lips tease the shell as he fully situates himself between my thighs, that position pushing me right up to the edge, practically vibrating with need.

"You like this, mate?" he whispers, his breath warm over my ear and sending chills dancing on my oversensitive skin. He slides in another inch, one hand on my hip, the other massaging my breast.

"Yes," I breathe the word.

"And this?" He slides in another inch, hot and hard and filling me so much I can barely breathe or think around needing more of him.

"Stars, *yes.*" I glance down at Tor, wondering if I can hold myself up with just one arm long enough to properly touch him. The sight of him beneath me, eons of carved muscle, pumping himself in the way I should be, has me aching even more.

"You want us to fuck you, Cari?" Steel whispers, still at my ear, and I *shiver* at the way he says it, the primal dominance in it.

"Yes," I answer. I want to be devoured by these two, consumed until there is nothing left. They're leaving. They're leaving and I won't be there to make sure they're okay. And this moment between us is stretching on a millisecond of eternity, one we may never get to capture again, which makes each sensation a thousand times more potent.

"Then open that pretty mouth of yours," Tor says, and I whimper at the command.

The effect of these two glorious males is intoxicating, reducing me to nothing but *theirs* as they have their way with me.

I part my lips, lowering my mouth over Tor's cock at the same time Steel sinks all the way inside me. My moan ripples around Tor's cock, the vibrations making him hiss as he thrusts his hips off the floor.

Steel rises up on his knees behind me, slowly gliding in and out of me, each time more heated than the next. He's dragging it out, claiming me in brazenly long strokes that have my entire body shaking.

I relax my jaw, opening wider as Tor fucks my mouth, each thrust speeding my heart as he fills me. I relish the warm taste of him in my mouth, and moan as Steel grips my hip, holding me steady as he ups his pace, giving in to his own needs as he takes me harder.

*Stars*, these two.

Every inch of me tightens, coiling like a heated spring ready to snap. Every graze of Steel's free hand over my back, between my thighs as he pumps into me, is like striking a match. Each thrust from Tor, each graze of his cock along the edges of my teeth as he claims my mouth is like a ticking clock on a bomb ready to blow.

"*Cari*," Steel groans when I push back as he thrusts in, meeting him harder, faster. "Fuck."

I swirl my tongue around Tor's head, closing my lips around him and sucking as he glides in and out, devouring him as he did me moments ago.

Steel's grip on my hip tightens, his other hand pressing against my spine until my breasts brush Tor's thighs as I continue to take him in my mouth.

My senses soar, the bonds between us sparking to life with each thrust, stroke, caress. Everything heightens between us as we submit to the needs of our bodies, our bonds, and as my orgasm climbs and climbs, I'm fully and irrevocably lost in my mates.

They're lightning and strength, challenge and heart, and I simply can never and *will* never get enough of them.

I moan around Tor's cock, unable to control myself as Steel slams home again and again while rolling his fingers over my clit until I come apart completely.

My body shakes with the throes of it, with the intensity of my orgasm as I clench around Steel's cock, drawing his own release from him.

*"Wife,"* Tor warns, but I don't dare pull away. Don't move as he comes inside my mouth. I swallow him down, only pulling back when he's finished, my jaw tender from taking the full length of him inside me.

Steel gently pulls out of me, and I collapse atop Tor, who easily shifts me to the side, propping my head atop his muscular chest. Steel slides in behind me, slowly gliding his fingers over my arm and hip and back up again.

"Admit it," Tor says. "We gave you something to think about while we're gone."

Steel laughs. "You're going to miss us."

"Always," I say, the reality of the situation making my chest tight. "But just to be sure," I say propping myself up and shifting until I'm standing above them, walking backward toward the table. "How about you give me a little more to think about?"

The two stand, both glorious and wholly different as they stalk toward where I tempt them from the table. And as they descend on me with kisses and languid touches, I pray to the stars to stop time, to stretch this moment into a forever that war can't touch.

# 11

# LOCK

*C*ari has been quiet the entire flight to the Air Realm. We left the Fire Realm the minute the extra ships showed up, one of them to collect Tor and Steel. Their goodbye hangs heavy between the three of us, but I spotted Blaize's ship trailing after them—he walks the line of madness I love to dance with, but he's never let Steel down before. And it offers some comfort as we head into the unknown minus two of our strongest allies.

"Darling," I say when she hasn't stopped staring at a spot on the metal table in the gathering area of the ship. It's just me and her. Talon's in the cockpit, guiding the ship to the Air Realm.

Cari blinks and looks up at me. "Do you think it will be in ruins?" she asks. "Like the last two?"

I can feel the worry rippling down our bond, feel the blame she's already wrapping around herself. I move from my seat, settling next to her and tucking her into my side. "We're almost there," I say instead of answering. The odds aren't in the Air Realm's favor, not after what we've seen. "It's out of our control."

Normally, I'd delight in the chaos of it all, in the unpredictable nature of the ruthless Shattered Isle king. But not this time. Not when there is so much innocent bloodshed. Not when it pains my mate so damn much.

Her thoughts and memories are so loud I can't help but hear them, see them play out in my mind as if they belonged to me. Memories of her suffering as a youngling, struggling to be the stealthy killing machine her father wanted her to be. Flashes of assassins her age or three times it, fighting her, beating her, judging her.

Anger rises, the itch to slice my shadows into someone is fucking overwhelming. I close my eyes and breathe deeply, clenching my fist against my knee in an effort to quell the urge to kill and slaughter and maim for what my mate has suffered. Anyone who had a hand in it, in her tragic uprising, in the brutality of her training. I'll slice into their minds, paint their worst fears with a master artist's hand until their panic consumes their soul—

"Lock," Cari says, her hands on my cheeks as she climbs into my lap. "You're shaking."

I open my eyes, noting my shadows have blotted out almost all the light in the room, cocooning us in darkness.

"You may not want to sit so close, darling," I say through clenched teeth as I try to reel in my power. I've always struggled to control the chaos within me, the instant urge to repay injustices against me or those I love with ten times the pain in which they were delivered.

She holds my gaze, staying right where she is, perched with a knee on either side of my hips, her hands on my face, eyes on me like I'm something to be cherished, not feared. "I'm not afraid of your rage," she says, and I shudder beneath her. "I trust it."

She could've said *I'm not afraid of you* but she knows I would never harm her—she's wise enough, knows me well enough to label my rage as something not entirely in my control.

I blow out a breath. "Fuck, I love you," I say.

She leans closer, brushing her lips over mine in a tender way that speaks more to my current needs than her own. Gentle, cautious, almost timid, the way one would approach a wild animal.

With each graze of her lips over my own, a tightened piece of me uncoils, until I can finally move my hands without the fear of my shadows slicing into the closest living thing—my mate. I wrap my arms around her back and hold her tight against me, chest to chest, nose to nose as I look her in the eyes.

"Whatever this venture brings," I say, stopping only to kiss her again before pulling back. "We face it together."

She kisses me again instead of responding, almost as if she knows she can't make that kind of declaration.

I jerk back, cocking a warning brow at her. "Promise me, Cari," I say, her name rolling off my tongue instead of the pet name I like to play with. The severity flickers in her eyes, and she visibly swallows as she slides her fingers into my hair.

"We face it together," she says, then slams her mouth against mine so hard it hurts, and fuck me, I love the way it stings. My mate is ice and passion and hunger and power, my match in every way imaginable. Even as I know she's lied to save me before, I don't have the strength to call her on it now.

I need to believe her, in this moment, with death surrounding us, because the thought of anything happening to her, of any harm falling upon her…

Another lick of anger heats my blood, but my mate senses it, and pushes me against the bench, harder, more demanding as she rocks against me. "Stay with me," she pleads, knowing I'm about to spiral again.

"Always," I sigh between her lips, kissing her back as unforgivingly as she is kissing me.

I splay my fingers along her spine, holding her against me so no breath of space is between us. There is only me and her and the heat building between us. We're fully clothed, something I only now realize is terribly inconvenient as I rise, hefting her along with me. "Oh look," I say, drawing my lips away from hers long enough to speak. "Another table."

She grins against my mouth, her legs locked around my waist as I walk us toward it.

"How do you keep finding yourself in these predicaments with me, darling?" I ask as I place her atop it, leaning her back so I can run my hands along her thighs, relishing the luxurious feel of her fighting leathers beneath my fingers.

Cari arches into my touch. "I suppose I only catch you when you're hungry for me," she teases, her voice breathy from our kisses.

"For you?" I ask, kissing my way down her neck and back up her jawline. "I'm always starved." I slide my hand between her thighs, teasing her over her leathers.

"Same," she says, her breath hitching as I increase my pressure, stroking her until I can feel the heat pooling there.

"How is that possible?" I ask, claiming her mouth again for a moment before pulling back. "How can this need between us be so equal, so matched?"

"Maybe we were born lucky," she answers, and our eyes clash together in a moment of truth that has us both freezing.

We weren't born lucky. Both of us know that down to the scars we still bear from our upbringing.

Her lips part, a shaken breath escaping as if she can take the words back.

I shake my head, smoothing back some of her hair, and press my forehead against hers. "Perhaps," I say, kissing her gently. "The events from our past that left us scarred were merely treacherous little stepping stones that led us to each other."

She spears both hands into my hair, bringing her mouth a breath away from mine. "I love you too," she says before kissing me again. It's timid at first, languid and sensual and filled with all the love between us.

But it soon turns frantic between us, edged with need as sharp as my favorite shadow-blade. We're a clash of teeth and tongues as we hurriedly reach for the other's pants—

"We've landed," Talon's voice is like a bucket of ice-cold water splashing upon us both.

My shadows skitter away at my brother's presence, revealing Cari and myself in all our compromising glory upon the table. Sure, we're fully clothed, but something flashes in Talon's eyes that is equal parts jealousy and threat and need.

"Perfect timing, dear brother," I chide him, but shift us so Cari is on her own two feet again. She straightens her shirt where it had hiked up to reveal her soft blue skin, and I note the way Talon's eyes linger there.

Another time, I might've invited him to join us—she's his mate too, after all—but I know in this moment, I know something Cari needs more than the pleasure I can wring from her body.

The safety of the Air Realm.

So I wave an arm at Talon and say, "Lead the way."

\* \* \*

"We've been over this for the last hour, your highness," Lady Celeste, the leader of the Air Realm, says from where she stands before us, clad in a gown made up of the royal colors of the Air Realm—whites and blues and silvers. "I have no intention of siding with the Shattered Isle king. I do not support his endeavors."

"And yet when we landed, your soldiers were gathering supplies and your citizens were taking all preparations for war," Talon says from where he stands across the room of her personal council chambers.

Cari has remained quiet and contemplative as Talon takes the lead in the questioning. I have too, keeping myself busy with tunneling through the Air Realm leader's mental shields to hunt for deception.

"We are at war, are we not?" she asks, then adds with a sweet smile. "Your highness?"

"Yes," Talon says, a growl low in his chest.

"Then why wouldn't I be preparing? News has reached us of the attacks in the Earth Realm and Fire Realm. We do not intend to be taken by surprise."

Talon glances to me, and I dip my head. There isn't a hint of deception coming from the leader, and luckily for her, there isn't a wisp of flirting behind her smile, lest my mate chop her to bits. No, there is nothing but a solid amount of respect and loyalty radiating in her mind, and it helps ease the growing tension in my chest.

We have allies yet in this war.

"Thank you for seeing us," Cari says, reaching out to shake the leader's hand.

"I wish it were under better circumstances, my queen." She bows a little after releasing her hand. "I know you visited one of my smaller cities on your last journey through here. I would've liked to have met you then."

"I agree," Cari says, flashing the leader a genuine smile. "Maybe when this is all over, we can have a proper introduction, one with more drinks and food and less war strategies and warnings."

The severity of that statement dumps ice on the warm way the conversation was building, but they both take it in stride as the leader focuses her attention on me and Talon. "You have my word that we will support you in this upcoming war, if you should have need of us. In the meantime, I trust you'll grant us the permission to defend ourselves as we see necessary, and the preparations that go along with it."

"Of course," Cari says, and Talon and I nod our agreement.

"Is there anything you need from us now?" the leader asks.

"We'll need to stay here for a little longer while we make preparations for the next part of our journey," Talon says, not revealing the exact location of where we're headed. Good, as much as I trust this leader, I want zero rumors making their way back to the Isle and ruining our element of surprise. "We'll depart soon."

"You're always welcome to stay as long as you like." She bows again, and we thank her before filing out of her council chambers, navigating the long hallways of her mansion and onto the streets of the Air Realm's capital city.

"How long are we staying?" Cari asks once we've hit a steady stride walking among the business district. She's eager to fly. I can sense it in her voice. And I understand, especially since this realm is not under direct attack.

"A little while longer," Talon says as we navigate the busy streets, eying businesses as we go.

I hold back a smile, remembering it was a neighboring city where I found Cari, scented the bonds on her, felt my own drawing me to her, and held her mind for only a moment, as to allow my brothers to capture me. Funny, I was certain that plan would lead to my father's death, but I had no idea it would lead me to the love of my life.

"I want to put feelers out for the state of the Shattered Isle before we head that direction," Talon says. "Want to hear from Gessi and connect with Steel and Tor to see how they're faring too. This may be our last chance to do so before we cross into enemy territory."

Cari's eyes find the pavement, her pace slowing to a near stop among the crowded area. People file around her, and Talon and I spin around to face her. I'm prepared to tell her *enemy territory* doesn't encompass the good and noble people she loves, but I quickly note she's not offended by what Talon said. No, she's laser-focused on something down an alleyway between two towering buildings that nearly scrape the sky.

"What is it, darling?" I ask.

"I feel something..."

Before we can take two steps toward her, she races down the alleyway in a bolt of speed. My heart climbs into my throat at her pursuit, Talon and I snapping into motion a second after her, close on her heels.

She clambers atop a garbage receptacle and leaps, her hand extended, ice crystalizing along her fingers as she grips something.

"Cari!" I yell as we watch her hurtle toward the ground, a dark mass in her grip that had blended into the building before.

The mass is four times her size, the shape of a male but rippling with obsidian power, like Talon's suits of armor, but this is no machine. This is some living, breathing kind of power that has my shadows snapping to attention.

Cari presses her knee against the thing's massive chest, and it bares razor-sharp teeth at her from where it lays beneath her.

Talon's armor is already covering his body, and my shadows are at the ready as we flank her left and right.

She's staring down at the creature, not breaking the gaze of the two glistening orbs staring back at her.

"I win," she says, shocking the hell out of me and Talon, if the look on his face is any indication. She removes her knee, climbing off the creature, and arches a brow at it. "I'm guessing since I'm still breathing, you weren't sent here to kill me. *Varian.*"

A deep, rough laugh rumbles from the creature, and the obsidian around it shifts and snakes inward, revealing a male in Shattered Isle garb.

Cari extends a hand toward him, and he takes it, using it to help him stand—he towers over her.

"You've gotten better," he says, teal eyes scanning the length of her body in an assessing way, not a sexual one—otherwise he'd have no eyes remaining to look.

"I've been better than you for over a decade, Varian," she fires back.

He laughs, shaking his head before glancing at me and ignoring Talon completely. He steps past Cari, eyes on mine as he sizes me up. "You have a problem, shadow spitter?"

I furrow my brow, leaning to cock a brow at Cari. She rolls her eyes, coming to stand at my side.

"Varian," she says. "These are two of my mates. Lock," she points to me, "and Talon." She motions to Talon, who's come to stand behind her, armor still on. "Varian is one of the deadliest of the elite Shattered Isle assassins. We've trained together since we were younglings."

Varian shifts his weight, almost like he's preparing for a fight.

"And the thing that roams beneath his skin?" I ask.

"Intimidated?" Varian smirks, showing a little of the beast behind his eyes.

"Should I be?" I ask, calm and cool on the outside, my shadows already sharpening their claws on the inside.

"Absolutely," he says without hesitation.

Cari steps in front of me, the move making me look to the sky to search for patience.

"Varian," she says, all playful reminiscing gone from her tone. "Why are you here?"

He shrugs. "Hunting. What else?"

"For me?"

He scoffs. "Sure, that's what the general's orders were."

Talon and I move as one, but Cari throws her arms out, stopping us. "If he wanted me, I'd already be gone."

I gape at her, but she shrugs too. "No use lying. I've seen him in action."

"Yeah," he says, smirking. "She's seen me in action."

"I will put you back on the ground," Cari warns, and it's our turn to laugh.

Varian nods, then folds his arms over his chest. "I'm not after you," he says with sincerity, and I finally have a modicum of respect for the creature. "Payne thinks I am. But you know we've never seen eye to eye."

Cari nods. "Who are you after, then?"

"I'm checking to see how many here are weaponing up against the SI," he explains. "Wanted to confirm rumors. Our numbers are slim on the island, thanks to Payne. You know his methods. Anyone strong enough to stand up to him is terrified on their family's behalf." A muscle in his jaw ticks. "Came to the elemental realms to round up some rebels."

Cari blows out a breath. "Gessi said you were on a mission—"

"You asked about him?" Talon growls.

Varian laughs, then rolls his eyes. "She's not wrong," he says. "Doesn't change the fact that she's being reckless." He eyes Cari. "I thought you of all people would've talked her out of the assistant-to-the-general gig."

"I tried," Cari says, raking her fingers through her hair.

"Yeah, well, maybe next time you talk to her, try harder. She's going to get herself killed."

"You think I don't know that?" Cari snaps, her anger and fear for her friend flaring across the bond.

Varian steps into her space, which is only allowed because Cari is still motioning for us to stand down. "Killing her would be a blessing, a gift bestowed upon her by the general," he says, and Cari shudders. "You *know* what he'll do to her if he catches her doing anything that questions his authority."

Something like true terror flickers in his eyes, but it's gone in a blink.

Panic buzzes down our bond, and I graze my hand over Cari's lower back in support.

"I know," she whispers. "We're almost there," she says, and Talon clears his throat.

Varian rolls his eyes. "Easy there, tin can," he says, eying Talon's armor. He pushes past Cari, then myself and Talon, before turning around at the end of the alleyway. "I'm one of the bad ones," he says. "That doesn't mean I'm the worst." He eyes Cari. "You work your angle, and I'll work mine. Hopefully, by the time we see each other again, we're both giving

Gessi a lecture that will make her think twice before she gambles with her life." He winks at Cari before shifting into the obsidian beast, clawing his way up the walls of the building until he's out of sight.

Cari blows out a breath, her eyes trailing after him.

"Can we trust him, Cari?" Talon asks, his armor clinking back into the buttons on his palms.

"Honestly?" She glances between us both. "I have no idea."

# 12

# TALON

"*E*nhance." I stand with my arms folded over my chest, eyes darting between the four screens I have up on the monitors in the control room on River's ship. Mine would've been about ten times faster, but I have to say, River has some nice tech outfitted on his ship.

The video from the surveillance drones I sent out last night shakes off its fuzzy quality with my command, showing a different portion of the Shattered Isle royal city on each screen. I furrow my brow, leaning closer to the second screen where the drone is broadcasting live, its focus on the palace itself.

"Is that…" Cari's voice sounds from behind me, and I don't bother turning around. She's at my side, eyes wide as she examines the screens.

I scan her face, noting the tension in her jaw, the glittering tears in her eyes as she looks at what used to be her home. It still can be her home, I suppose, in a way, but not until she finishes this war with her father, with the general.

I continue watching her, seeing the shift from the vulnerable princess, who is conflicted about her home, to the ruthless assassin who knows the mission matters above all else. Her spine straightens, the moisture clears from her eyes, and she blows out a breath as she points to screen three.

"Those are the coves with passages to the palace my father knows about," she says.

I nod. "I'm guessing those guards and sky ships aren't normally there."

"Never," she says, shaking her head as she moves to examine screen number four. "Damn it."

"Looks like General Payne is a little more paranoid about an outside attack than your father ever was, or it's simply the circumstances of the past few weeks that have made him position units all over the royal city," I say, rubbing my palms over my face. "This changes things," I continue.

Anger flickers in her dark eyes, her lip curling. "Bastard," she says, then moves to the first screen. "There's no sign of any random sky ships? Non-Shattered-Isle ships that my father may have stolen and returned with?"

I shake my head. "None that I've seen, but the drones have only been transmitting for a few hours. We'll have to watch the royal city for a few days, most likely. Learn the rotations of the guards, ensure we won't be seen when we slip into the coves and tunnels you and Gessi created in secret."

Cari smacks her palms against the control panel, turning her back on the screens as she rakes her fingers through her hair. "I can't just *sit* here, Talon. I need to move. To act. I'm restless." Her eyes meet mine, pleading. "Every second we waste is another chance for my father to attack another defenseless city or realm. Another chance for him to turn the realms against you and your brothers' rule."

"*Our* rule," I correct her, stepping into her path when she's started pacing.

I wave my hand toward the screens, but keep my focus on her. "This is a snag we didn't expect. I agree. It's frustrating as hell, but if we storm in there right this second, we will be taken down. The general has enough guards patrolling the royal city to catch anything amiss. They're not going to miss their princess returning home, especially if she's kicking in the front door."

She eyes me, but there is a levity there that helps me breathe easier. The last thing I want is for Cari to disappear in the night, embarking on a solo mission to stop this war without us. She'll do it too, if we don't watch her. She feels all of this is her responsibility—which, of course, I can relate to—but she can't face this alone.

"We will study this *diligently*," I continue. "I already have an algorithm running to note routine schedules and any changes in the rotations. The second we spot a hole in their system, we will strike. I promise you that."

The tension loosens a fraction in her bunched shoulders, and she rolls her neck as she breathes deeply. "And in the meantime," she says, glancing at the ceiling like she's searching for answers. "I'm supposed to just sit here and wait?"

Anxiousness flutters down our bond, the nervous energy settling under my skin. I glance back at the screens, then lean over the controls, typing out commands at rapid speed. The devices on the back of my hands beep, and I turn around to face Cari again. "All done," I say, and she tilts her head at me. "I've uploaded the information to my portable units," I say, showing her my hands as I lead her out of the room. "If something changes, we'll know right away."

"Okay," she says, allowing me to walk her toward the gathering area of the ship. "So now I get to sit in my chambers all day and wait?"

I shake my head. "The Air City capitol is a peaceful city, not to mention it has spectacular food. Let's feed you."

She gapes up at me. "You want to go out to dinner? In the middle of…all that's happening?"

"We can't make a move on the palace right now," I say. "There are no signs or rumors of your father's whereabouts. Steel contacted me earlier, saying he and Tor are almost to the All Plane with no hitches. Lock is off stalking Varian in the shadows to see if he'll be an ally or not." I shrug. "We have to eat, so we might as well do it somewhere nice."

A slow smile shapes her lips, the sight so rare lately that it makes my chest expand. I put that there. In the midst of all the guilt and regret and worry she has, I have the ability to make her smile. And I intend to keep putting it there, throughout this all.

"Will you join me?" I ask, extending my arm to her.

A few weeks ago, I wouldn't be caught dead anywhere near her, let alone begging her for one-on-one time. I assumed she'd just as quickly sink a knife in my back then eat with me. But honesty and mating bonds can change so much in so little time.

Cari loops her arm through mine. "Last time we had dinner together in a city, I had to save you from getting your head chopped off. I believe I was poisoned in the process," she teases as we walk down the loading bridge and toward a main city street near the sky ship-bay.

Anger slices through me at the memory, at the way I'd thought she'd been trying to kill me, when she'd been my savior. And with the way I'd treated her? She could've let me die and no one would've been the wiser. I'd hated her, and she'd hated me. There were times even now we disagreed with that level of passion, but it didn't matter. She was mine, and I was hers.

"That won't happen again," I say, my voice low, sharp.

"You know you can't control everything, right?" she asks as we walk along the pathways near the center of the city. Air Realm citizens are out in full force as the sun sets, hustling from one place to the next, creating an excited buzz that is infectious.

"Have you met me?" I fire back, my eyes cutting to hers.

"Oh, I've met you all right," she says, rolling her eyes. "And I know you feel like you have to predict every outcome, know every exit strategy, but history has proven that isn't possible."

"Doesn't mean I'll stop trying," I say, turning toward a restaurant I've visited in the past. I hold the door open for her, motioning for her to go inside.

She stops before me, her chest grazing mine, sending bolts of electricity scattering over my skin. "You might need to, Talon," she says. "Or else you'll miss all the things that happen when you aren't preparing for the worst."

I cock a brow at her. "Like what?"

"Like *life*." She brushes past me, and I follow her in, my throat tightening at her words.

Minutes later, we're seated in the highest portion of the building. Our table is tucked against a wall of floor-to-ceiling windows, the evening sky a smear of orange and yellow with white fluffy clouds scattered across it. Cari is smiling as she watches the sky, noting the lavender birds that swoop in circles or fly in flocks outside our window.

"I can see why this is your favorite spot in the capital," she says, leaning back in her seat after we've ordered our food.

I gaze out the window, nodding. "Everything is quieter up here."

Cari sips her sparkling wine before setting it down. "You get that way when you fly, don't you," she says, nodding toward the devices on the back of my hands.

The two inventions are of my own making that transform into a suit of armor around my body. I didn't have Steel's inherent strength or Tor's elemental abilities, and I certainly couldn't control and read minds or manipulate shadows as Lock does. All I have is my mind, and I'd be lying if I said I didn't use that gift to satisfy my own desires.

"Who doesn't want to fly?" I ask, sipping from my drink.

"People who are afraid of heights."

I narrow my gaze at her. "You're not afraid of anything," I say. She'd proven as much when she accepted her mission to kill us, then accepted the demands of her heart to love us and stand against her father, against my father. My mate is fearless, in ways that are admirable and terrifying.

"I fear things," she says, but shrugs. "I was simply raised in a world where fear was unacceptable." Her eyes go distant, some memory from her past tugging at her. It passes in a few blinks. "I once showed how scared I was of Varian," she says.

I straighten at the mention of him, at the way the beast that lurks beneath his skin had surfaced yesterday. The fear that streaked through me when Cari had faced him without a hint of worry for herself. He's formidable, even I can admit that. I sensed the power radiating from him the second Cari shucked him off the building. It's the exact reason Lock is tailing him now. We can't risk a foe like him going unchecked for too long, and since Cari herself didn't even know if she can trust him, he's a threat until proven otherwise.

"We couldn't have been over twelve," she continues after our food has been delivered. She moves her steak around on her plate with her fork, lost in her story. "He had yet to master his powers, master that beast he turns into."

"He was volatile," I say, and she nods.

"What youngling isn't?" She shrugs. "Especially when forced to wield and hone that kind of power? I could barely have an emotion without nearly slicing someone's head off with my ice, and Varian?" A shudder runs through her. "It was almost as if the beast was a separate entity who controlled him as opposed to the other way around. And one day, under General Payne's orders, we were sparring with our powers and I accidentally sunk one of my tiny ice daggers into his arm. We always tried to draw the least amount of blood possible from the other, but I slipped."

My chest tightens, acid boiling in my stomach at the picture she's painting.

"Varian transformed," she continues. "More than he ever had before. A full transformation with the beast growing Varian to three times his normal size. The skin a morphing obsidian that could hardly be wounded, and those teeth…"

Her voice trails off, and I remain silent, remembering with clarity the razor-sharp teeth. They were the last thing I'd want sinking into my flesh.

"I was terrified," she admits. "I managed to fight him off, and the general ended the session. But he'd *seen* my fear and reported it to my father." She sighs. "I no longer trained with Crane or anyone my age after that. Just Varian."

My hand curls into a fist on the table. "Say the word," I say. "And I'll kill him."

She laughs, shaking her head. "It's not Varian's fault," she says, and I tilt my head at her. "In fact, he has every right to hate me. To want me dead—"

"No one has that right," I cut her off.

"He does," she says anyway. "The general forced him to transform, to fight me, to tear into me, over and over again. Many times the general threatened to kill him if he didn't comply, and there were so many times he was sent to the dungeons because he couldn't shift back." She visibly swallows. "They'd trap him behind bars until the beast let him go and he was himself again." She shakes her head. "For years, he was subjected to that torture. *Years*. All because I showed a natural reaction of fear to a ruthlessly powerful predator."

A modicum of sympathy unraveled for Varian, but only a tiny percentage. "That's a terrible situation, for sure," I say. "But he's directly linked to a tragic piece of your past, so I'll never be able to get along with the guy." I shrug. "Plus, all those trials likely sharpened him into the weapon he is now. He seemed fully in control of his powers yesterday." Which is why Lock and I decided to have Lock tail him. There are too many unknowns surrounding him, and with that kind of power? Fuck me if he decided to unleash it on the people of this city.

"The result doesn't erase the darkness used to buy it," she says.

"I know," I agree. "But we can't change our pasts, Cari. We can only change the choices we make in our present. Those are the things that define a creature, whether good or bad or everything in between. Varian has the free will to choose how he lives his life, and those choices have nothing to do with how he was raised or how you tied into it."

She purses her lips, contemplative, before she finishes her plate of food.

An hour later, our server clears our drinks, bowing slightly. "I apologize, your majesties, but the restaurant is now closing because of the new city-wide curfew Lady Celeste has implemented."

Cari and I share a look, but nod and leave enough money for the bill and a sizable tip. I guide her out of the building and onto the city streets, both of us immediately noting the shift in the last two hours. Before, it had been a bustle of excitement and energy, and now, shops and stores are closing, people are hurrying into their homes like a violent storm is heading their way.

In a way, I guess there is a storm coming. But one of blood and teeth as opposed to wind and rain.

"Well," Cari says as we board our ship, no sign of Lock anywhere. "Thank you, Talon. That managed to distract me for a whole two hours before the curfew reminded me of what we're waiting on."

The attack on her father, her home. "I wish I could make time move faster for you," I say, walking her to her room. "I wish I could figure out the best time to strike and set you loose."

She cracks a small grin as we stop outside her door. "Are you saying I'm your prisoner here, Talon?" She walks her fingers up my chest. "Because it looks like my hands are free to do what they want."

"I can tie you up, mate," I say, shifting closer to her. "If that's what it takes to keep you here. To keep you from making plans without us."

Her lips part, shock flitting through her eyes. "I would never do that—"

"You would," I say, walking her back until her spine is against her closed door. "You know you would."

She tips her chin up defiantly, and need ripples down the bond between us. I see what she needs. I sense it as it mixes with my own. More distraction while we can do nothing but wait. If I'm being honest, I need it desperately too when every instinct is screaming to study the Isle until my eyes bleed, until I can find a way to finish this.

"Go ahead," I say. "Try to lie to me and say you wouldn't. I dare you."

Her throat bobs, a shiver running the length of her body that is flush with mine. But she doesn't deny it, doesn't try to lie to me.

I tilt my head, grazing my fingers along her neck and down the center of her chest, teasing the outside of her breast over her gown. "Tell me, mate," I say, eyes on her. "Do you want to be my good girl tonight or my bad one?"

Her breath hitches as I inch my mouth toward hers, and I hold us there, the anticipation stretching between us like a rope ready to snap.

She bats her eyelashes at me, the picture of dangerous innocence before she smiles an assassin's smile. *"Bad."*

The word rips through me, shifting my need to adjust to what she wants from me, what she wants me to take from her.

Her control. She doesn't want to bear the weight of it for one more minute.

Well, I can handle that, handle her.

"Open the door," I command, lacing my tone with all the dominance and authority I possess. She wants to me to take the reins and I'm more than happy to be what she needs, to slip into these familiar roles between us.

She opens the door, and we stumble inside her room. I close and lock it behind me, leaning against it. I slide my hands into my pockets and nod toward her. "Take off your clothes."

Every time I issue a command, this little flicker of heat flares in her eyes that has my dick hardening, aching to sink inside her, but I'm going to take my damn time.

Cari reaches behind her, unclasping her dress before she lets it pool at her feet. She steps out of the silk, her beautiful body now only hidden by scraps of black lace. I take my time trailing my gaze over her breasts, her curves, down to her bare toes. Her rich blue skin is supple and soft and begging to be touched, but I remain where I am.

"All of them," I say.

A shiver runs through her, but she sheds the lace, baring herself to me.

Sun damn it all, she's a vision.

A temptation and a cure.

A promise and a challenge.

She's everything I never knew I needed.

"Don't move unless I tell you to," I say, pushing off the door and walking toward her.

I roll up my shirtsleeves to the elbow as I walk in slow circles around her, my eyes a caress over every inch of her body. Her breath heightens with each circle, the anticipation stretching our bond taut.

Stopping before her, I unbuckle my belt, sliding it through the loops, and folding it in half. Her eyes flash as I glide the folded leather down the center of her chest, teasing it over her hips before reaching the apex of her thighs. My cock hardens at the memory of this belt marking her delicious ass, branding her as mine the first time we were together.

I press that folded leather between her legs, rubbing the hard surface against her clit, every muscle inside me tightening as her eyes flutter with the sensation of it. Watching her submit like this, when I know how powerful and deadly she is, is one of the sexiest things I've ever seen. And the fact that she *wants* to submit to me? It's almost too much, making me want to lose the game and fuck her senseless against the wall right this second.

But that's not what she needs.

She needs distraction.

She needs time to stretch where she's not worried or carrying the weight of this war.

And I'm always going to give her what she needs.

"Talon," she breathes my name, her hands flying to my chest as she rocks against the leather.

I pull it away from her, and her eyes fly open in question.

"You moved," I say, a dark spark flickering through my blood at the game we're playing. I walk around her, and lightly crack the belt over her beautiful ass.

She gasps, arching slightly from the move, but quickly rights herself.

I do it again, and a moan tears through her lips, but she doesn't move.

"Good girl," I say, rounding her to stand in front of her again.

Pleasure is churning in her eyes, and I can feel the bead of precome on my cock from how badly I want her, how much I'm enjoying watching her like this. I unbutton my pants, kicking off my boots and shedding the pants seconds later, baring myself to her. I eye my hard cock, noting the wetness there.

"On your knees," I demand, and she instantly drops before me. I have to clench my jaw to keep from groaning at the sight of her there, naked and kneeling before me. "Lick that off," I say. "I want to see those pretty lips around my cock."

She grins up at me, leaning forward and wrapping her lips around me in an instant. Her tongue swirls over my head before she sucks me deeper into her mouth, and I groan. My grip on the belt in my hand tightens as I lose myself in the sensation of her, the way she's bobbing up and down, licking and sucking. Her hands are on my thighs, exploring and digging her nails in just enough to make everything inside me tighten.

If she keeps this up, she'll ruin all the fun.

"Stand up," I demand, my voice rough.

She whimpers slightly as she pulls me out of her mouth, a satisfying little popping sound happening as my cock is freed from her lips. *Fuck*, I want her.

I scan the room, noting a bar for hanging towels is on the door near her bathing chamber. I walk her over to it, not giving myself the pleasure of touching her just yet.

"Hands up," I say once she's beneath the bar.

She slowly draws her hands above her head, and I smooth my free hand up her arm, relishing the feel of her silky skin under my fingers. I unfold my belt and wrap it around her wrists, securing them above her head and to the bar before I step back to survey her.

"Stunning," I say, eyes roaming every inch of her. "Feel free to move now," I say.

"You tied me up," she says, breathless. "How am I supposed to move?"

I smirk at the tease, and move forward, flicking one of her nipples. She gasps as the small hurt pebbles it, and I do the same to the other one before leaning over slightly, sucking one into my mouth to soothe it, and repeat the motion to the other.

The leather creaks as she tugs against it, wanting to touch me, but unable to because of the restraint. I pull back, catching her gaze before I glance down to where she's rubbing her thighs together.

"Need something, mate?" I ask against her lips, biting down gently before sliding my tongue into her mouth, relishing her moan as she kisses me back.

I pull back, tilting my head at her.

"Yes," she says.

"Tell me what you need."

"You," she says instantly.

I shake my head, taking a step back. "Tell me exactly what you need."

Her lips pop open, and she shifts under her restraints again. "I need you between my thighs," she finally says.

"Good," I say, taking a step closer. I slide my fingers between her thighs, stroking her wet pussy in slick glides and teasing circles. "Like this?" I ask, and she nods, her eyes closed. I dance around her entrance, sliding through her wetness, stroking her without ever going inside, working her until her breathing is rushed and she's rocking against me, trying to get me where she needs me.

"Talon," she groans, her eyes on mine, churning with need and frustration as I wind her up. "I need more," she pleads.

"Tell me how much more."

"Your fingers," she says, breathless, as she rocks against me. "I need them inside me."

I shudder, heat licking up my spine, my cock hardening to the nth degree as she takes ownership of her needs. I reward her by plunging two fingers inside her, pumping her while I flatten the heel of my palm against her clit.

"Stars, *Talon*." She rides my hand, her arms flexing against the restraint. "More, please," she begs. "More."

I slant my mouth over hers, kissing her hard before jerking back. "More, what?" I demand.

She groans, frustration coloring her tone. I still inside her, my knees nearly buckling at the feel of her pussy fluttering around my fingers.

"More, what, Cari?" I demand. She'll ruin us both if she doesn't answer me.

"Surprise me!" she says, capturing my mouth, crushing her lips against mine in a fierce kiss that has me growling.

I pump her again, and she moans between our kiss as I slide my other hand over her hip and around to the small of her back. I trace my fingers over the curve of her ass before smacking it slightly, loving how she bucks against my other hand from the move.

"Yes," she sighs, riding my hand while I explore her with my other.

I draw my mouth from hers, just far enough so I can watch her reaction as I slide my finger down the seam of her beautiful ass and between her cheeks.

Her eyes flare wide as I explore the tight area, teasing it while I pump her relentlessly from the front. Over and over again, I pump and thrust and tease her from both sides, until she's trembling, until she's bucking and soaking my fingers as she comes.

She goes limp against me, and I gently slide my fingers out of her, hurrying to unbutton my shirt, tossing it over my shoulder so I'm as bare as she is. Sweat beads on both our bodies, and her eyes are lust hazed and hooded as I step up to her.

I snake one arm around her lower back, her breasts teasing my chest as I bring us flush. "I'm going to fuck you until you can't stand up on your own."

Cari whimpers as I spread her thighs with my leg, and lift her, lining my cock up with her slick, swollen pussy.

"I own every inch of your pleasure now, you understand me?" I slide in an inch, my cock aching to sink into the hilt. "I'm going to make you come whenever and however many times I want."

Her breath hitches as I slide in another inch. Her searing heat hugs my cock like nothing else, and I have to grind my teeth to keep from unleashing on her entirely.

"Now," I say, holding us both there in the torturous anticipation. "Tell me you understand. Tell me who you belong to."

"I understand," she says, rocking her hips in an attempt to get me fully inside her.

"And?" I ask.

"And," she says, her thighs trembling as she tries to move on me. "And…"

"Who do you belong to?" I demand.

"You," she says, crushing her mouth on mine before pulling away. "Talon," she says. "I belong to you."

"Fuck right you do," I say, then slam inside her.

Her head rocks back, her arms pulling tight against the restraint as I do it again.

I wind both arms around her lower back, lifting her so I can fuck her from a deeper angle, her breasts bobbing from how hard I thrust into her.

"Talon, I'm..." She loses track of her words, her body trembling, her pussy clenching my cock as she can do nothing but hold on as I pound one orgasm into another, her body sparking at each stroke, each thrust.

"Stars," she moans, her hands yanking at her restraint. "Talon, please," she begs. "I want to touch you. Please let me touch you."

The hungry desperation in her voice has me holding her with one arm, reaching up with my free hand and undoing the restraint with one move. She throws her arms around my neck, the force of her embrace nearly knocking me off balance. She moves, pushing on my chest until I comply, dropping us to the floor. She doesn't stop our pace, doesn't miss a beat as she straddles me, riding my cock so fast and hard I see fucking stars.

"Cari," I groan, my fingers biting into her hips as she takes full control. She's a beautiful, stunning, wild creature above me, every inch the powerful assassin who owns her pleasure and chases what she wants.

Fuck, she *picked* me. Was *made* for me.

She's so slick atop me, the sounds of our bodies joining together fill the room, and my release builds and builds until the strain is so tight I'm sure I'll snap any moment.

"*Talon,*" she moans, her pussy fluttering around my cock with another orgasm, and it's the shove I can't stop as we plummet over the edge together. I piston my hips from underneath, pounding her through my orgasm and hers, our breaths matched in speed, our bodies slick with sweat as she collapses against me.

I hold her there against my chest as we come down, as we return from the orbit we'd been in. Sun damn me, we could've been the only two creatures in the realm for how wrapped up I am in my mate.

As her breathing evens and her muscles relax, I gently maneuver us to stand, but her legs tremble enough that she tilts slightly, an exhausted laugh on her lips as I scoop her up and carry her to the bed.

"Told you, you wouldn't be able to stand straight," I say.

"You did promise me," she says, eyes lined with exhaustion as I tuck us into the bed. She lays her head on my chest, and I absently play with her hair as the sounds of her breathing shift toward sleep.

"I always keep my promises," I whisper long after she's fallen asleep, which evades me because all I can hope is that I truly can keep my promise to her and end this war once and for all before it kills one of us.

Because I know with absolute certainty, neither myself nor my brothers will survive it if our mate is lost.

## 13

## CARI

*T*wo days.

It's been two whole days watching Talon's stealth drones. Two days of studying the patterns of the guards and looking for a break in their regiment. Two days and still no word from Gessi, and I haven't dared ask CB-1 to contact her for fear of revealing her position.

I think I hate the waiting most of all. I'd rather be in the battle, actively doing something, rather than sitting here waiting for someone else to attack. Waiting for my father to make a move. It feels like a dark chess game and I'm merely a pawn on my father's board. The longer I wait, the longer I feel like that little girl, desperate for my father's approval and working myself to the bone, shaping my mind and body into an unmatched weapon, only to be told I'll never meet his expectations.

CB-1 whirs next to my ear, the little floating sphere nudging against my neck. I blink out of the daze I'd fallen into from staring at Talon's screens for hours.

"At least I've learned some things," I tell the little robot, who blinks his blue eye at me. I motion toward the screens. "General Payne takes a walk through the royal city every night at three," I say. "And he takes a great deal of his personal guard with him."

Including Crane. I spotted the male easily enough—we'd trained enough as younglings for me to make him a mile away. The leathers, the eyes that are sharp as a hawk's, the way he moves with such graceful precision it's almost as if he's flying. Cheeky bastard can sneak up on anyone, including me, which made for extremely hard training sessions, back when we were allowed to train together. Back before Varian was used against me so much.

"He likes to reinforce his position on those walks," I grumble, wishing I could be in one of the establishments he frequents nightly—the taverns or gambling halls. Wishing I could cloak myself well enough to catch him by surprise and sink an ice sword into his chest.

"No sign of my father," I continue. "Where are you?" I mumble to myself, my mind spinning like the spokes in a gear, churning and turning without ever getting to the finish. Steel and Tor are almost to the All Plane, but have seen no signs of him. There have been similar attacks on their borders, according to Storm and River. I find it hard to believe my father would waste his efforts singularly on testing the borders of the All Plane, not when he could be using that time to gather followers to aid him when he officially declares war against us.

He's recruited some Corters from the Fire Realm—that much was clear during the battle—but how? Unless we truly had just missed him, like Gessi had suggested. Or perhaps he didn't need to be present to have followers flocking to his cause. The Fire Realm has been known to disagree with the All Plane on numerous political matters. Maybe they see my father's open attacks as a way to satisfy their disagreements and bring upon a new era.

Again, to what end? What does my father expect to gain from these random attacks on the realms? He has to know the All Plane will never bend to him. They've barely accepted me and I'm *mated* to their kings.

Me. The Shattered Isle princess is now the queen of the All Plane.

*Stars save us.*

A drop of ice water skates down my spine. I sit up straighter in my chair, CB-1 following the movement, staying at my side.

"I need to find Lock," I say, rising from my chair and hurrying out of the ship, CB-1 sliding around my neck. Talon is in a meeting with Lady Celeste, discussing any irregularities she's seen the last two days, so I can't interrupt him. And Lock has made it his personal mission to stalk Varian, day and night, to uncover if he can be trusted or not, but I need him. I need to talk to someone about what I just realized.

Fear makes my feet move faster, and I ignore disgruntled looks as I hurry through the crowded streets, dressed simply in cotton pants and an All Plane shirt, my hair tied up on my head in a top-knot. Surely, I look mad with the way I'm storming about the city, hunting for my mate as the sun sets and the curfew is about to be implemented across the city, but I don't have time to care about upholding queenly images.

I dive inward, wrapping myself around Lock and my bond and yanking on it.

There.

I can smell his snow and stars' scent. Can feel his shadow's caress as I follow the direction the bond leads me. I wind through main streets and buildings before I stop in front of a local gambling hall. Shoving through the doors, I'm immediately met with the smell of flavored air—a popular commodity in these cities. Establishments sell the stuff by the canister in flavors ranging from lavender to cinnamon to citrus, and it supposedly gives the user a feeling of euphoria for a short period of time. Maybe, when the war is over, I'll buy a case of it for me and my mates to experiment with, but since I need all my senses to win this war, I don't dare entertain indulging now.

Colored lights illuminate the gambling hall, complete with three marble bars offering everything from liquor to sparkling wine to the flavored air. The main floor is packed with creatures delighting in the bets taking place at various table games, but the bond leads me upstairs, to where balconies overlook the main area.

"And then I made them believe they were falling with no end in sight," Lock's voice sounds from across the room, and I follow it, finding him laughing with Varian, the two seated at a full table topped with hunter green felt, and playing cards in each of their hands.

Varian smacks his hand on the table. "Is that right?" he shakes his head, tapping his temple. "And they never knew the truth?"

Lock is grinning like a cat who's just nabbed a mouse. "Not even a hint. They died where they stood, their hearts giving out from the strain of it."

Varian visibly shudders, then tosses his cards toward the dealer sitting at the center of the table. "And they say I'm a monster," he says, but he's laughing again, and so is Lock.

I note the amber-colored drinks before them, the stacks upon stacks of chips collected in front of them, and can't help but wonder how long they've been here. Anger bubbles to the surface at the ease between them, the aloofness they have when all this time I've been walking on eggshells, studying how to get to my Isle—

"Darling!" Lock says, his voice rising as he waves me over. "Look at how many units I've won."

I arch a brow at him, rounding the table to stand between where he and Varian sit.

Varian points at Lock, drink sloshing in his hand. "This one here is quite the shadow," he says in a deep, raspy voice before he hiccups. "Finally convinced him to play cards with me instead of stalking me from the darkness he likes to bathe in."

"I thought you were on assignment," I whisper-hiss to Lock, unable to hide my anger. I'm about to fall to pieces and he's playing cards with someone who could or couldn't be our enemy?

"I was," he says. "I *am*." He eyes Varian with a little more clarity, and I tilt my head at him.

"Come on, Cari," Varian says, using my name with a sense of familiarity I haven't heard in years. It was always *princess* after the general pitted us against each other. "Take a seat.

Let me win some of those All Plane riches from you. For the cause."

I eye the full table, the other players flashing smiles or nods in my direction.

Lock pushes back in his chair, patting his thigh. "This seat is always yours," he says, and I gape at him before spinning on my heels and heading out the direction I came in.

"Uh oh," I hear Varian say as I reach the stairs. "Trouble in paradise?"

"Cari!" Lock calls, but I'm already racing down the stairs, my heart pounding in my chest and ice trickling into my veins. I know it's irrational, but Lock has been absent these past two days, all for the sake of his mission. I needed him I find he's playing cards and getting drunk with Varian?

I make it through the doors of the gambling hall before shadows gather around my body, tugging me into an alleyway between the two brick buildings. Lock's scent invades my senses, quelling some of that misplaced rage as he manifests behind me.

"Why are you upset with me, darling?" he asks at my ear, and I melt into his embrace for a few moments before I take a step away and turn to face him.

"You've been gone," I snap, my body shaking with adrenaline. "Following Varian while I have to sit and watch those cameras, praying for a chance to strike—"

"I told you that you need only call, and I'd return," he says, eyes narrowed on me as I pace before him. He slides his hands into the pockets of his hunter green coat. "You never have. I assumed you were well taken care of."

I swallow hard. Of course, Talon had been extremely attentive the last two days, almost as if he felt he needed to make up for the absence of his three brothers, but still.

I stop pacing, folding my arms over my chest, and practically hiss at Lock when he smiles at the move. "You seem to be awfully chummy with your *target*," I snap.

"Varian?" he asks smoothly, playing the cool, calm, collected card when I'm practically spitting fire. "Truly, an interesting creature. Funny, even, in a dark, sadistic sort of way." Lock shrugs. "He made me the first day I started tailing him. So, I took a different approach. The male loves to chat after a few whiskeys."

My shoulders drop. "What did you learn?"

Lock *tsks* me. "No, darling, I'm not sharing with you until you share with me."

I sigh, shaking my head. "Lock, please. No games today. I'm—"

"This is no game," he says with all seriousness, stepping into my space. He towers over me. "You're angry with me, and I think I deserve to know why."

"I'm not angry—"

"I can *feel* it," he cuts over me. "Tell me."

"I'm not angry with you!" I yell, my fingers shaking at my sides as tears well in my eyes.

Lock is silent, his blue-green eyes imploring as he takes another step closer.

"I'm angry with *me*," I admit on a breath. "I realized it today," I continue. "Just now, back at the ship. It's why I came to find you. I...I..." The words tangle in my throat, adrenaline coursing through my veins as my body begs me to fly, to fight, to do something other than stand here nearly crying and doing nothing to help the situation at hand.

"What is it, darling?" he asks, hands gently clutching my shoulders.

I look up at him, shame slicking over my soul like an oil. "My father, he may not have gotten what he wanted when I fell in love with you all," I explain. "And he may have lost his partnership with your father, but he has something now he didn't have before."

"What?"

"Me," I say, my voice cracking. "He has direct ties to the queen of the All Plane. Lock, don't you see?" I shake my head, pushing out of his embrace, needing to move before I burst. "He's my father. Everyone knows that. And those who know about our strained relationship are *rare*. The attacks on the realms, the looks I've been getting everywhere we go? His actions are directly affecting how the realms view their new queen." I blow out a shaken breath. "And now I'm of more value to him than I've ever been before. I'm a queen with four mates who will do *anything* for her." Terror grips me, the ice-cold fingers of fear scraping down my spine. "And he knows I'll do anything for you four, too."

A muscle in Lock's jaw ticks as the pieces come together for him.

"Don't you see it? All he has to do is get ahold of any one of you, and he'll have the queen at his mercy."

"We won't allow that to happen," Lock says, his words sharp, determined.

"He's already succeeding!" My breaths come in ragged gasps. "Steel and Tor are already separated from us. The realms are in disarray. And you're likely questioning our marriage's worth this very moment. He's winning," I say, my chest heaving as panic climbs to clutch my throat. "He's winning, and he's barely even trying—"

*"Listen to me,"* Lock's voice slices through the panic swirling in my mind, stopping me in my tracks. He steps into my path, hands on my cheeks as he forces me to look at him. "You," he says the word out loud. "Are not just a pawn in your father's schemes," he continues. "You're not just my wife or an arranged marriage between our two fathers. You are not even just my mate." His eyes scan my face, looking at me as if I'm precious to him, and my heart aches with the intensity of that look. "You are my everything, darling," he says, and tears roll down my cheeks. He swipes them away with his thumbs, drawing me closer. "You're my stars in an endless night sky, my sanity in a sea of madness, my chaos in the midst of normality. There is not a force in this universe that could *ever* make me question my love for you."

I close my eyes, and he wipes away more of my tears.

"All the realms can turn against us for all I care," he says, and I open my eyes, focusing on him again. "And I will still love you. I will stand by your side as we fight every single creature who tries to tear us apart, do you hear me? Nothing and no one will ever take you from me or me from you."

I throw my arms around his neck, and he hauls me up to his level, allowing me to cry it out, to shed the weight of the emotions I've held in these past days. My revelation earlier about what power my father now has over me sent me spiraling, and Lock manages to soothe every worry and hurt with a few words.

I lean back enough to brush my lips over his. "My stars in an endless night sky," I repeat his words, and he nods. The love in my heart expands so much I can barely breathe around it. "Take us somewhere?" I ask.

"Where do you want to go?" He grazes the tip of his nose over mine.

"Anywhere I can be alone with my mate," I say, and shadows instantly burst around us, swirling until our feet lift off the ground. I cling to Lock even though I know he'd never drop me as he whisks us up higher and higher until I'm not sure where the ground is.

"Is this alone enough for you?" Lock asks once our feet touch something solid. The shadows melt from around us, revealing the freshly dawned night sky surrounding us in all directions. A blanket of midnight and diamonds every way I turn.

I fold my hands over my chest as I slowly turn in a circle on the roof of some infinitely tall Air Realm capital building. We're so high up there isn't a hint of noise, nothing but the sounds of our breathing.

"Lock," I say, turning to face him. "This is...everything," I finally say. "It's everything."

He grins at me, eyes flickering from me up to the sky. He points at a section of glittering stars, three of them shining brighter than the others around it. "What is the name of that constellation?" he asks, and my gaze widens on him. He smiles down at me and shrugs. "I've always loved the stars. Even when my father tried to beat it out of me." He shakes his head. "I never understood his strict doctrine, the way he believed something as pure and beautiful as this..." He points to the stars. "Could ever possibly unlock portions of our mind and turn against us." He rolls his eyes. "Only someone who has no understanding of the mind would spit such lies."

I reach for his hand, interlocking my fingers with his, my heart breaking for what he endured as a youngling. For what his father subjected him to just because of who he is, what he could do, and what he enjoyed.

"You haven't spoken about him," I say, squeezing his hand. "Since you…"

"Killed him?" he finishes for me.

"Yes," I say. "You know I would understand if you needed to talk about it." Killing your father is certainly a theme among me and my mate, but I have no idea the internal repercussions of that action. Lock does…

"You think I would be mournful," he says, shrugging. "Feel some flicker of regret or guilt." He shakes his head. "I don't. Maybe that makes me a monster, but the male I grew up knowing was never the one my brothers knew. There was no love for me in his heart, or for anyone for that matter. The long years had twisted him into something I don't believe even he recognized." Lock sighs. "He died the minute he ordered hits on my brothers."

I nod, understanding clanging through me as the memory of my father's hand around my throat soars through my mind. "Mine is dead too," I say. "He just doesn't know it yet."

Something flickers in Lock's blue-green eyes, his long dark hair blowing slightly in the breeze.

I swallow around the lump in my throat and point to the constellation he asked about earlier. "That's the hunter," I say. "Our legends say he fired a bolt so hard from his bow that he split the rest of the stars up, scattering them across the night so the entire universe could enjoy them."

"And that one?" Lock asks, walking to the other side of the roof and pointing to another constellation whose stars are twinkling in the shape of a cup.

"That's my favorite," I say, walking to stand next to him.

"Why? What do your legends say about it?"

"It's the star's representation of water," I explain, tracing the connections with my finger. "See how it looks like a cup dipping into a stream?"

"Ahh," he says. "Yes." He turns, smiling down at me. "Your realm is of water, your power is of the element."

I nod, and he tugs me down to the roof, splaying us both on our backs. "Tell me more," he says.

And so I do.

I tell him about the stars I grew up loving. I tell him about the constellations the All Plane fear will unlock minds and unleash evil. I tell him how powerful they are, but only to the ones who believe in them.

We talk until the sting of earlier doesn't burn anymore, replaced wholly by the love for my mate who understands me to the roots of my soul.

Lock holds me on the roof as silence settles between us, his touches along my arm growing more languid with each graze. I roll to my side and he mimics me, our eyes locking.

"Now you know," I say. "How there is nothing to fear from the stars."

"Oh, I don't know about that," he says, and I laugh.

"Is that right? Do you feel your evil has been unlocked because you've looked upon them, studied them for more than an hour?"

"Certainly not," he says. "But the lies spread about them and the people who live beneath them…those are dangerous."

"People are always more dangerous than legends," I say.

Lock reaches between us, smoothing his hand over my cheek. "Do you want to go?"

I shake my head, shifting closer to him. He wraps his arms around me where we lay, until my head is on his chest, and he's playing with my hair that he's freed from its tie.

"Can we stay a little longer?" I ask, not ready to let go of this moment he's carved out just for the two of us. This perfect piece of quiet amongst the stars, hidden on the top of an Air Realm building where no one will stand a chance of finding us.

"We can stay up here forever," he says, planting a kiss atop my hair, holding me a little closer to him.

And I can't help but entertain that fantasy, even for just a moment, when reality is so much more complicated.

## 14
## STEEL

"This is where the last attack happened?" I ask River as we slow our hover bikes near the western border of the All Plane royal city.

"Yep," River says. "We managed to save the guard on duty. She'd been strangled, but our soldiers got to her in time. She's recovering in the military infirmary."

I crouch down, running my fingers through the lush green grass where he indicates.

Storm is briefing Tor back at the palace on what all we've missed since we were gone, but I wanted to get to the latest attack scene the second we made it back home.

Home. It doesn't hold the same ring to it, not while Cari is a world away.

I've been separated from my mate for six days now, and I can feel that distance like an ocean opening up in my soul, raging and chaotic.

"There were no signs of the attacker?" I manage to ask, standing back up as I scan the area. The guard's outpost is about thirty feet to our left, a little bunker of stone packed with weapons and food and even a little cot for longer missions.

"None," River answers. "Even the guard couldn't remember who attacked her."

I furrow my brow. "So, either she didn't see it coming or…"

"Or the attacker is a ghost," River finishes for me.

"There is no such thing—"

"I know," River cuts me off. "But that doesn't mean that killers can't become invisible."

I nod at that, because he himself could use his tech to shrink himself to near invisibility. "You don't know of anyone with tech like yours, right?"

He shakes his head as we head back to the hover bikes. "Nope. I keep my plans encrypted and have fingerprint access only to all my gear. So, unless someone came up with their own and kept it off the radar…" He shrugs and throws a leg over his bike, as do I.

"Which side haven't they hit?" I ask as we start up the bikes.

"Northern," he answers.

The closet border to the palace.

"All right then," I say, my guiding my back around in a circle.

"All right then, what?"

"I'll be taking over guard duty in the northern sector tonight," I say before taking off in that direction.

\* \* \*

"I'm just saying," Blaize says from where he sits perched atop a counter inside the northern border's guard bunker. "The guy's an asshole."

"*Hey.*" I snap my gaze up to him from where I stand watch at the tinted window. "That's my brother."

Blaize shrugs. "And he's always been an asshole."

I sigh, closing my eyes for the briefest of seconds. "Talon is... Talon. You're the two who have history—"

"And you think he'd cut me some slack after everything that's happened."

"He might," I say, turning to face him. "If he gets a chance to process all that's happened. We have barely had a second to fit into our crowns, let alone deal with the death of our father, the betrayal..." My chest tightens, but I shove the pain away, focusing outside the window again.

We've been on watch for a few hours now, dressed in standard royal guard uniforms, as if we were any other All Plane males on a shift to protect our beloved royal city. I'd told Blaize he didn't have to come, but Blaize does what Blaize wants, and luckily for me, that usually means watching my back.

"All right, all right," Blaize raises his hands in defeat, then hops off the counter. "I'll drop it." He walks over to my side, noting the quiet night outside. "How are you handling being away from your mate, then?"

I look at him, mouth parted as I shake my head.

"What?" he asks.

"Can't you ever, just once, talk about something that isn't painful?"

He shrugs. "Would you like me otherwise?"

I huff a laugh, then return to focusing out the window. "Being away from Cari is like..." I search for the right words. "Like being submerged under water. I can't breathe without her."

Blaize whistles. "That's rough," he says. "I know you were born for the whole mate thing," he continues, and I arch a brow at him. "But I'm not cut out for that level of dedication."

I crack a grin. "You're pretty dedicated to me."

He smiles at me, hands splayed over the center of his chest. "If only you were fated to be mine," he teases, then rolls his eyes. "I've never met a soul who I'd want to hold that kind of power over me. The kind of strain you're going through right now? It's dangerous. Can make you sloppy."

"Did you just call your king sloppy?" I fire back, a laugh on my lips.

"I told you on day one, I'm *never* calling you king. You're already cocky enough."

I smile, shaking my head at my friend. I've missed him, and it's always easy like this when it's just the two of us. If Talon is in the mix, they fight like snakes trapped in the same cage.

"Regardless of what you think," I say. "You won't be able to resist when the time comes. The right person?" I shake my head. "The bonding process is overwhelming. You'll want that person more than your next breath. Even Talon, who hated Cari when he first met her, succumbed to it. That's how it works."

Blaize shakes his head. "Thank the sun it's rare," he says, his eyes widening as he looks outside the window.

I follow his gaze, spotting the almost imperceptible movement just outside.

We share a silent look, then nod to each other as I go out the front door, and he slips out the back.

The night air is cool and crisp, the smell of grass and soil wafting on the breeze. In this section of the border, the All Plane land stretches on for miles, the only building in sight the guard bunker. Lush grasses blend into the night sky on the horizon, alluding to a solitary sort of existence, but I can feel it…someone or something is here.

I walk slowly, disguised in the royal soldier uniform, strolling as if I'm just out for some fresh air during my long night shift. Something prickles at the back of my neck, an awareness that sends icy chills over my skin.

Adrenaline courses through my veins, but I keep my breathing even and calm as I examine the stars. I've never truly looked at them for too long or with any more interest than that of passing something beautiful—our father always insisted that they'd capture my mind if I studied them too long. After marrying Cari, I know how ridiculous that is. My father gave the stars power by making them off limits to our people and he let his own fear of losing control of his realm eat away at his mind until nothing else good or decent was left. Maybe all that died with my mother. Maybe he'd always been cruel, and we'd never been able to see it. Either way, the stars most certainly couldn't be blamed for his behavior or that of any other evil entity.

All my senses stand at attention as I feel a swipe of wind slash at my back—

A loud *thunk* rattles the silence, and I spin around just as a blade drops at my feet.

The male wielding the blade drops to the ground too, thanks to Blaize, who has tackled him from behind.

I scan the area, searching for any other enemies, but it's just him. He struggles under Blaize's weight, his image flickering in and out of sight as Blaize jerks him to his feet.

"Get him inside," I say, chest heaving as I follow them inside the guard bunker.

Blaize forces him into a chair, shackling his arms and legs to it.

"What is your name?" I ask once Blaize falls back to my side.

The male spits at my boots.

I sigh, shaking my head as I crouch down before him. "We can do this the easy way or the hard way," I say, glancing over him. He's well built, clearly from the Shattered Isle with black hair spiked up in a row down the center of his head, and the emblem blazoned across his chest. A fluttering sound fills the room, and he flickers in and out of sight again. "That's a neat trick," I say, standing again. "You used it to kill several of my soldiers. They never saw you coming."

The male flashes into sight again, his powers only that of invisibility, not teleportation, for which I'm thankful. He's secure, and I've got all night to break this son of a bitch. "There are more of me," he says, yanking against his restraints.

The chains tighten around his wrists and ankles, and he bites back a scream.

I nod to the restraints. "My brother's invention," I explain. "The more you struggle, the tighter they'll grow." I glance to Blaize. "You remember the time that Corter we caught attacking innocent females wouldn't listen to us about these chains?"

Blaize doesn't take his dark gaze off of the male. "Yeah," he says, arms folded over his chest, his silver tattoo glittering underneath the lights in the room. "He lost several of his limbs that day."

The male blanches.

"Let's try again," I say. "What's your name?"

Nothing.

"Who sent you?" I ask, but he remains silent. "I can assume from the moon and stars emblem over your chest that you serve the Shattered Isle king."

The male visibly swallows.

"Are you trying to accomplish something by killing my soldiers?" I pace before him. "Or are you just bloodthirsty?"

He laughs then, a sadistic, no-remorse laugh that scrapes my nerves raw. "You don't scare me," he says, shaking his head. "I've studied your history. You're weak. Always treating your prisoners with care and kindness, feeding them, trying to enlighten them." He rolls his eyes. "You may as well let me go. I know you'll never cross your lines. Not like we do. We know how to get things done on the Isle, and soon enough, you'll learn that too."

I sigh, raking my palms over my face.

"You're right," I say, giving him my best smile. "I don't cross lines." I glance to Blaize, who is still staring down at the male with barely held disgust. "But he does."

The male's eyes fly wide as Blaize rushes him, backhanding him with his silver hand. The crack shakes the room, and the male whimpers as he spits blood on the floor.

"You're going to have to kill me," he says. "I'll never tell—"

"There are so many ways to keep you alive though," Blaize cuts him off, one hand gripping the male's hair, the other a fist connecting with his jaw. "We have healers who can mend every broken bone and almost every ailment. I can tear you apart over and over again," he explains, punching the male twice more. "And put you back together again every day. We can do this for years." He leans close, eying the blood dripping down the male's face as he gives him a malicious grin. "And I'll relish every scream, every cry for mercy. I love breaking people. So, hold out as long as you like. You'll be doing me a favor."

Blaize cracks the male across the jaw, back and forth, the male's head swinging left and right. He hits him so hard he falls back in the chair, but Blaize doesn't stop. He leaps atop the chair and keeps pounding the male until even I flinch from the blood splatter.

I reach out my hand, grabbing Blaize's shoulder and urging him back. His knuckles are split and his chest is heaving as he pushes his dark hair out of his face. There's a hint of madness in his eyes, that same sense of rebellion and rage that has always made Talon wary of him.

He meets my eyes, and nods as he backs off.

I haul the male upright, cringing at his swollen face. "Want to go for round two? Or do you want to give me something so I can convince my friend over there to stop beating you?"

The male slumps in the chair, his eyes not fully focused as he looks at me. "The king," he says, his words garbled by his mouthful of blood. Some of it spills down his chin and onto his chest. "You did exactly what he wanted."

My chest tightens. "What?"

The male huffs. "He wants his daughter alone. Separated from you. And here you are. Tor too, from what I hear." His teeth are outlined in blood when he smiles. "And he has something the princess wants," he says, eyes closed. "Something she'll do anything for."

I tilt my head, and Blaize steps up behind me. The male flinches, whimpering at the nearness of my friend. "Call him off," he begs. "I told you—"

"You haven't told me anything," I snap.

His split lip trembles. "Kill me," he whispers. "Just kill me. He will if you don't. If he finds out I told you."

"Who will? The king?"

The male shakes his head. "He'll watch. The general. He's in control now."

I furrow my brow. "What does the king have that Cari wants? What is he going to try to get her to do?"

Apprehension climbs up my throat as the male focuses on me. "The king wants to use the princess's new position as queen. Wants to wield her as a political weapon to get her to join the kingdoms and name him king of all the realms beyond the All Plane."

I swallow hard. Cari's position as queen afforded her the luxuries of appointing new leaders to the realms whenever she liked, only protected by the fact that all four of us had to approve her choices. And we'd never approve that, we'd never allow the Shattered Isle king to rule, and Cari would never suggest such a thing. Even if the king held a knife to her throat. Unless…

I grip the male's shirt, jerking him closer to me. "Who does he have?"

Silence.

"Who does he have?"

Nothing.

"Blaize, loosen his tongue."

Blaize takes one step forward, and the male breaks out in a sob.

"He has the princess's handmaiden. Her best friend," he blurts out. "Gessi," he says, his body shaking. "The general has Gessi, and he plans to kill her if the princess doesn't do as they ask."

I shove away from the male, curling my hands into fists as I keep backing up until I'm outside.

"Steel," Blaize says, coming to stand before me. "Who is Gessi to Cari?"

I meet his gaze. "*You*," I say, and Blaize flinches. "She's to Cari what you are to me."

And the only other soul beyond me or my brothers she'd risk everything for.

"I have to contact Talon." I whirl toward my hover bike, needing to get back to the communication towers in the palace. "Can you handle him?"

Blaize smirks at me. "I know how to deposit a prisoner to the dungeons," he says, a gleam in his eye.

I arch a brow at him. "In one piece," I order.

Blaize shrugs. "That's up to him."

I nod, then start the bike. "Meet me when you're done."

Blaize nods, then goes back into the bunker while I race toward the palace, wondering the whole time how I'm going to tell Cari.

Because the second she finds out, she'll rush off to save her friend with no regard for her own safety. I can't keep this from her, but I can't condemn my mate to die, either, and since she's already so close to the palace, I can't stop the fear from climbing up my spine, screaming at me that it's already too late.

## 15

## GESSI

*A*s far as prison cells go, mine certainly isn't the worst on the Isle.

The slick rock walls are the color of midnight, and they are considerably larger than many of the other cells that crowd beneath the palace above. Chambers that are filled with innocent Shattered Islers who simply had the backbone to speak out against General Payne.

I curl my hand into a fist where I sit on the meager cot that is attached to the wall farthest from my cell's door. I'm so far away from those innocents that I can no longer hear their screams. It should be a small comfort, but instead, I'm shamed by it.

Working as the general's assistant these past weeks has been profitable in the information I've been collecting and sending my dearest friend, Cari, but it's also been pure torture. Not the kind the general has taken pleasure in since hauling me here two nights ago, but the kind that eats at my soul every second I can't save our people. I've had to stand idle and emotionless and watch as he imprisons more and more good people, only because he fears an uprising so much he practically stinks of it. I've envisioned the ways I would kill him if I could, but he's conniving and malicious, and when he attacks, he goes for the *hurt*. Which is what he's doing to me now—harming innocent people rather than taking out the full punishment on me.

I'd rather be in the smaller cells with them in the even lower levels. Rather be enduring their cries of pain and pleas for help than be stuck *here* where I have a barred window that shows me a slice of the night sky. The others...they don't have the luxuries I do. And yes, the general has taken it upon himself to bruise nearly every inch of my body, but he hasn't come close to breaking my spirit. The others? I fear they may never recover.

A crisp, earthy scent overpowers the dank mildew smell of my chamber, thanks to the makeover I've given it. Little touches from my powers—a lush carpet of spring grass over the jagged rocks of the floor and a wooden chair carved specifically for my body when I tire of the cot.

I glare up at the smooth rock wall on the right side, near the cell's door. There are metal hooks there and chains still stained with my blood. I have green bruises all along my arms and stomach and legs, places he's touched me, marring my jade skin over and over again with no explanation as to *why*. He's never once brought up my correspondence with Cari, and I've been so damn careful.

I finger the necklace around my throat, the one I don't dare activate for fear of him discovering the truth, the one he's overlooked as a mere piece of my handmaiden attire. I need to get a message to Cari, but...

I cut a glance toward my door, my heart clenching. I can't see him, but I know he's there.

*Crane.*

The male I grew up with. The one with the eyes as green as fresh grass and as sharp as a hawk's. The one who didn't hesitate to throw me in this cell when the general ordered it.

I swallow the lump in my throat, damning my own heart for being so foolish. I thought our history would spare me, or at the very least, buy me an ally in this new predicament of mine. I'd been wrong. Crane is ever the Shattered Isle assassin he's been trained to be, and yet…there were so many times I thought I'd glimpsed something more from him.

That *more* had led me down a path of want and desire I'd never acted on, but has invaded my waking and dreaming thoughts. And now…now I can't even try to contact my friend for fear he'll see and report back. He never missed anything, never looked away.

I cross the room, examining the bloody chains, my body cringing from the memory of the general's grin as he tortured me. The same kind I'll endure tonight. Acid sizzles through my veins, but joy blooms in my heart like the buds on a vine at the thought of what will happen when Cari gets here. He will regret every touch, every bruise. My friend and I will spend *hours* ending him.

The cell door clangs as it's dragged open, and my heart races as the scent of dark spice and rose float in on a small breeze. Every nerve in me awakens at that smell and I can't help but inhale deeply—some inner, ridiculous part of me soothing at the scent instead of raging, like I should.

"Crane," I say without turning around, eyes still firmly on the chains. "Are you to be my tormentor tonight?" I ask, barely holding back a broken laugh. He's been my tormentor for far longer than the moment he threw me in this cell. The object of all my fantasies now turned into the fatal thorn in my side.

"Food," he says, his voice rough and low. "I brought you food."

"And you know I won't eat it," I say, now fiddling with the chains, if only to keep me from turning around.

A deep sigh radiates from behind me, and I hear him drop a tray on a small wooden table I'd constructed near my chair. He's brought me my meals every night I've been in here, but I've refused to eat it.

"So you're content to waste away?" he snaps, and it breaks me, his sharp tone.

I whirl around, eyes narrowed on him, and barely hide the breath I can't catch. Night's end, he's impossible in his suit of black leathers, hugging every muscle in his lithe body, his sandy brown hair cut short, those green eyes like emeralds as he holds my gaze.

"I'm content to not eat any of the poisons the general has you lace into the food," I finally fire back.

Something like pain flickers in his gaze, but it's gone in a blink. He crosses the distance between us, and I retreat until my back is against the wall, right next to the chains. A muscle in his jaw ticks, and his damn scent swirls all around me. I hate myself for wanting him as I have all these years. For wanting him still, even after he's betrayed me.

"You honestly think I would do that, Gess?"

A warm shiver races over my skin at the way he says my name, but I merely tip my chin. "You're the one who put me in here, Crane. No explanation. No pity. You tossed me in here and have stood guard at my door every night—"

"How do you know I've been at your door?" He tilts his head, his body nearly flush with mine. "You can't possibly see me—"

"Tell me I'm wrong," I say. "Tell me you aren't there every second. Watching. Waiting. Delighting in the torture the general doles out." I curl my nose at him, disgusted more with myself for having affections for this male when he clearly doesn't feel anything for me.

He slams a fist against the wall, just to the right of my face, and leaves it there, caging me in on one side. "You want me to be the monster, fine. It doesn't change the fact that you need to *eat.*"

I study him, confusion unfurling inside me at the way he seems so...annoyed by my not eating. As if he cares if I wither away or not. He's not once tried to stop the nightly torture, has never offered to set me free.

"What's it matter to you?" I ask, my voice a whisper between us. The need crying out inside me to breech the distance between us, to rake my fingers through his hair, to press my lips against his and find out what he tastes like is over-whelming. "If I wither away or not?" I manage to finish, shoving those incessant feelings down into a deep, dark place inside me.

His green eyes trace the curves of my face, the line of my neck, and lower before climbing back to my eyes again. "What's it to me?" he repeats, then shakes his head. "Gess—"

"See, your highness?" The general's voice cuts over whatever Crane is about to say. "I have her safe and secured, just like you asked."

Crane shifts away from me, folding his arms behind his back, slipping into the assassin mask he let fall moments before.

I swallow hard, then turn to see not only the general, but the Shattered Isle king standing inside my cell. Instinct has me falling to my knees in a bow and muttering "Your highness," as I remain there.

"I see you haven't lost your manners despite your living conditions," the king says, his voice a deep rumbling inside my chamber as he walks farther inside. "Rise."

I slowly stand, my eyes climbing and climbing to meet his. He's twice my height and has the strength of fifty males, and his telekinesis powers make him one of the most feared creatures in the universe. Or at least, he was before the All Plane king separated our Isle from the rest of the realms and cut off our connections to most technology and trade after The Great War. King Jerrick spent those two hundred years plotting his revenge and building an army alongside a secret band of assassins—to include his daughter—and now, time was up. The All Plane king is dead, and King Jerrick is in a prime position to make his move against the realms. I'd learned as much shadowing General Payne these past weeks.

The king circles me, tracing a finger over some of the bruises on my arms. It takes all the willpower I have not to flinch from that touch. He turns and eyes General Payne, who leans against the wall near the door, his spindly fingers tapping together as if he's eager to get to work.

"Not entirely safe, now is she?" The king arches a brow at the general.

The general shrugs, grinning that soulless grin. "Just ensuring she understands the severity of her situation, your highness."

The king grunts a response, then turns to look at Crane. "You're dismissed."

Crane hesitates, eyes flashing from the king to me and back again.

"Did you forget your place in my absence?" the king asks, and Crane blinks a few times before bowing and heading out of the room.

And I hate that little piece inside me that reaches for him, that silently begs him to come back, to not leave me alone with these two.

"Do you know why you're in here, Gessi?" The king's voice is kind and fatherly, the voice I remember from when I was a youngling and he would read the realm histories to Cari and me before bed.

"No," I say with as much an even voice as I can manage.

"You didn't tell her?" he asks the general.

"I thought you the best one, your highness," the general says.

"How long have you been friends with my daughter?" the king asks.

"Friends?" I ask, unable to hold back the shock. "We're not friends."

The general shoves off the wall, stomps across the chamber, and backhands me so hard I see stars. I palm my cheek, the sting mounting as I catch my breath and right myself.

A hissing sounds from outside the opened cell door, but I see nothing there.

"You will speak to your king like a proper female who knows her place, or I will cut out your tongue," the general snaps, raising his hand again.

"That's enough," the king says, and the general falls back.

"Explain," the king says to me.

I'm trembling and I hate that I can't stop it. Part fear for what is coming, part adrenaline. My powers climb, begging for me to overtake the stone in the walls and swallow the general whole, watch him as the stone crushes his lungs and makes his eyes pop from his skull. But the coward never comes here alone, and I have no intention of letting his guards or the Shattered Isle king kill me tonight.

"Cari is not my friend. She is my *sister*. She has been since the moment you placed us together when we were younglings."

A small, broken smile shapes the king's lips. "That is exactly what I wanted to hear."

My stomach plummets, and I check myself. The last thing I need is feeding into the king's plans, whatever they may be, but from the foreboding coursing through my blood, I fear I already have.

"She feels the same way about you," he says. "My daughter." His eyes find the floor and he shakes his head. "Her betrayal is a tragic one, for sure. But she was merely one plan in a hundred I've formed over the years. The centuries we've spent in exile. There is more than one way to bring a realm to its knees. I easily proved that when I planted the seeds of greed and hate in the All Plane king over the course of decades. His fall from grace was a slow process, but I managed it." He glances down at me. "You would've appreciated it," he says. "It was like gardening, which I know you love so much. I worked on that seed for years, tending to it, whispering to it, watching it grow until it bloomed and rooted so deep within the All Plane king that he became what he loathed most." He smiles then. "Me."

I swallow hard, but don't dare open my mouth as his brow shifts, anger contorting his features.

"But all that hard work, all that time, was wasted. His own blood ended him, and now I have to start anew. Luckily for me, I've tended other seeds as well." He focuses on me, pity flashing in his eyes.

The floor beneath my feet seems to fall out from under me.

"I don't understand, your highness," I say, opting for innocence, for weakness. "I've been a good handmaiden to your daughter my entire life. I've served the Shattered Isle my entire life—"

"Shush," he draws out the word, reaching down to cup my cheeks as if he still was that fatherly figure in my life. "I know you have," he continues. "Because I made it so."

I furrow my brow.

"There is only one thing that can rival the love of a mate," he says, and my heart stutters. "One bond that can compete with what the stars have declared." He grins. "A sibling," he says, and my knees shake. "Just as the All Plane kings would die for their brothers, Cari would do anything for you, of that I'm certain." He releases my cheeks and walks toward my cell door. "Including naming me the one true king of all the realms."

I gasp, and the general steps closer, snatching my arm in a painful grip.

"If she doesn't, well…" The king glances to the general, who nods and slams me against the wall so hard my head spins.

He hooks my wrists into the chains and then slams his fist into my side. The breath rushes from my lungs as he throws a punch across my face.

I go slack, but the chains hold me up.

"She will understand the meaning of loss," the king finishes, leaning in the opened doorway, content to watch as his general attempts to carve me to pieces.

# 16

# CARI

$\mathcal{I}$ head toward the cockpit, wanting a status update on how far out we are from reaching the drop spot on the Shattered Isle.

We studied the guard rotation for days and finally found a time just before dawn when the guards' shifts changed where we could fly in undetected. We had to be close, likely only a handful of hours out.

"What do you mean they have Gessi?" Talon's voice stops me cold as I linger outside in the hallway, the door to the cockpit just barely cracked.

"Blaize and I captured a Shattered Isle guard who'd been sent to kill our soldiers stationed along the borders," Steel's voice sounds over a speaker. "We got the information out of him an hour ago."

"Fuck," Talon says.

"You understand what this will do to our mate?" Steel asks. "This will break her. We can't let that happen."

"You're suggesting we keep this from her?" Lock says from somewhere in the room.

"I don't relish keeping anything from her," Steel says.

"Nor I," Tor's voice echoes across the speaker.

"But, Talon," Steel continues. "You know what she'll do."

My heart pounds against my chest, my cheeks heating as I stand here and listen to my mates discussing me.

"She'll go alone," Talon answers. "Just like the king wants her to."

I swallow hard, my fingers trembling as adrenaline skyrockets through my veins.

"We can't allow that to happen," Lock says. "She can't face him alone. We've been over this."

"I know," Steel says. "How close are you to the Shattered Isle?"

"Four hours," Talon says.

Four hours. My lungs grow tight. How long has my father had Gessi? What are they doing to her?

"You're that close?" Tor asks over the speaker. "Then wait until you land to tell her. Four hours will not make a difference."

But it does. It changes everything.

"I don't like this," Lock says.

"I don't either," Talon snaps. "But it's this or chain her up. That's what it will take to keep her from playing right into the king's hand. You know what he'll do to her—"

"It doesn't make it right," Lock cuts him off.

"Nothing about this is right," Steel says. "The bloodshed, the battles, the innocents being locked up on the Isle. It's all rooted in the king's selfish needs, his play for ultimate power. Cari is that power. She's the queen of the All Plane. And beyond us, she has only one weakness."

*Gessi.*

Steel isn't wrong. None of them are, truly. They know me to the very marrow of my bones. They know I'll never allow my father to use Gessi against me. Know I'd turn myself in before I'd allow that to happen. So, in part, I understand why they're having this discussion. If our positions were reversed, I'd do everything in my power to keep my mates alive, keep them safe, keep them smart.

"Lock," Talon says. "Do you still have Varian's contact information?"

"Yes."

"It's time to see if he's an ally or not," Talon says. "Maybe he's closer than we are. He doesn't have to wait for a secret entrance. Maybe he's made it back already and can help Gessi."

"I'll reach out now," Lock says.

I back away, as silently as I can, and hurry back to my chambers. I shut the door and give myself a few moments to collect my thoughts, to smooth a mask over my face and a mental shield hiding everything from the bonds inside me, so when they come for me, they'll have no idea I know. Not an easy feat, when mated such as we are.

I'll need to distract them. Thoroughly. I'll need them so focused on something else entirely that they'll stand no chance at seeing beyond my mask, at *sensing* my plans.

Pain lashes through my heart, torn between secrets and decisions I never wanted. But Gessi is like my sister and I will not leave her in the hands of someone as ruthless as my father and the general.

I blow out a breath, then smooth my hair back, sliding into the skin of the assassin I was raised me to be. A stealthy creature. A smooth liar. Someone who acts with strategy and power, not heart and emotions. A being as cold as the ice in my veins.

And only when I'm certain I can present a solid appearance, do I step out of my chamber and head back toward the cockpit. I knock on the door, which is now closed, and smile up at Talon when he opens it.

"Are we close?" I ask, almost horrified with myself at how smoothly my voice comes out. Not even a hint of the pain I feel wobbling a word.

"About four hours," he answers, and Lock steps behind him.

I can see it in his eyes, the battle. In Talon's too. They're both grappling for something to say to me, and my heart breaks all over again. Because there aren't supposed to be secrets between mates, not like us, not like this.

And it's not just them, I'm in on it too now. I plan to distract them, to protect them. Because if my father has Gessi...he won't stop there. And I will die before I let him get to my mates.

Alone.

The only way to win this is by being alone.

The only way an assassin works.

"Four hours," I say, sighing slightly. "I won't be able to sit still while we wait."

"Tell us what you need, darling, and we'll make it happen." Lock's blue-green eyes meet mine, and in that moment, I know I have them both.

"Distract me," I say, no *beg*. "Please?" I reach out my hands, one for each of them, and tug them down the hallway, toward my chambers.

A low growl rumbles from Talon's chest. "You know I don't like to share."

"I'm rather of that mind, too," Lock says.

I drop both their hands, opening my door and stepping through it. "You said whatever I need," I say. "And I *need* both of you."

Lock is the first one to step into my room, head tilted and eyes blazing. "Are you sure, darling?" he asks.

A lick of apprehension flares up my spine as Talon steps into the room and shuts the door behind him. These two... together? Steel and Tor and myself have found a rhythm that works for each of us together, but *them*? Chaos and punishment? Can I handle both at the same time?

Heat zips up my nerve endings, my core going liquid with the thought. Of course, I can handle them. They're my mates, and more so, I need them distracted and sated for what I plan to do next.

"Yes," I finally say, beckoning them both to the bed where I sit.

Talon and Lock share a look that makes me sit up a little straighter. They turn their focus on me, and the breath in my lungs catches.

"Ah ah, darling," Lock says, then snaps his fingers. Instantly, his shadows coil around me, dragging me to my feet and placing me before the two of them. "We don't come when you beckon." His wolfish grin shapes his lips, and lava shoots through my veins. "Where do you want her, brother?"

Talon's gaze rakes over my body, then scans my room as he folds his arms behind his back. "The chair," he says, nodding toward one of the cushioned chairs on the other side of the room. "Bend her over the back of it."

The shadows all around me lift me off my feet, settling me against the chair.

"I can move on my own," I snap playfully.

"Where is the fun in that?" Lock asks as he saunters over to me, dropping his coat over the opposite chair, and unbuttoning his long-sleeve shirt before tossing it too.

Night damn me, he's so beautiful. Scars and all, I love every single inch of him.

Talon pulls his shirt over his head, tossing it behind him as he walks over to me, gripping my chin and turning my face toward him and away from Lock as he leans down to slant his mouth over mine.

"Someone is jealous," Lock teases, his hands smoothing over the gown on my back as Talon punishes my mouth until I whimper. "It's okay, brother," he continues. "There are other places to kiss her."

I feel the sharp kiss of a shadow blade as it runs the length of my gown, the fabric melting away and pooling at my feet, leaving me completely bare to them both. Then Lock's hands are on my hips, gentle and teasing as he leans over me from behind, his mouth at my spine as he kisses his way down and down and—

"Lock!" I gasp as he yanks me down, away from Talon's mouth and away from the chair, until my thighs are poised over his head where he's now on the floor.

"Sit," he demands, and I can barely catch my breath from Talon's kiss, let alone process the new—"I said sit." He yanks me down, and my pussy settles right over his mouth. A moan escapes my lips, and my eyes drift up to Talon, who is glaring at his brother for stealing me from him.

Lock's tongue slides through the heat of me, his groan of delight vibrating against my sensitive flesh as he grips my ass and forces me to move on him. And after a few seconds, I submit wholly to the sensation, rocking back and forth on his mouth as he eats at me from below.

"Yes, darling," he says against my flesh, and I moan. "Ride my face."

I look down, a wild grin shaping my lips as I see Lock there—

Talon's hand finds my chin again, forcing me to look up at him. "Open your mouth," he says, and I shiver above Lock.

Talon's pants are gone, leaving him totally bare before me, his hard cock so damn close to my mouth. I flicker my gaze up to him, but moan when Lock thrusts his tongue inside me, stroking me with languid, heated laps.

Talon's grip tightens, parting my lips as he brings his cock right up to my mouth. "Did you hear me, mate? I want to fuck that pretty mouth of yours."

I'm breathless, rocking against Lock's mouth, my thighs trembling as he devours me. "Yes," I manage to say, and part my lips—

Talon plunges his cock into my mouth, and I moan around the taste of him. He's all heat and spice and stinging pleasure as he slides into my mouth all the way to the hilt. I loosen my jaw, adjusting to the size of him, and grip his hips while still balancing on Lock's face—but to be fair, Lock is controlling my body with his hold on me—and soon I'm a puppet to both of their needs.

I cast my gaze upward, watching Talon as he fucks my mouth, his hands in my hair as I bob up and down on his cock. My mind whirls, my body turning into a live wire from these two. Lock rocks me harder against him, and I abandon all sense of control as he licks me and his brother fills my mouth. My heart races, everything inside me narrowing to the feel of them, both their scents combining in a sea of snow and stars and leather and whiskey, creating something so new and invigorating I can hardly think around it—

Lock flattens his tongue against my clit, pushing me over the edge so forcefully my moans ripple around Talon's cock, my teeth grazing his shaft as he pumps into me, holding nothing back as he chases his own orgasm while mine is still ripping through me so hard my thighs tremble around Lock's cheeks.

"Fuck," Talon groans, spilling into my mouth without warning. I swallow him down, and he slides out of my mouth, smoothing his thumb over my swollen lips as I catch my breath.

Lock gently lifts me and moves out from under me, his shadows helping me to my feet in front of Talon.

Talon leans down, his mouth set for mine, but Lock turns my head before he can reach me, claiming the kiss for himself. The taste of me and him combines, and I go wholly liquid again.

A hand smacks my ass so hard I gasp, tearing out of Lock's kiss, only for Talon to claim it.

"Fucking hell, Cari," Talon groans against my mouth, his tongue sweeping in. "I can taste your pussy on your tongue."

Heat washes over me in a wave at his words, and another hand plunges between my thighs.

I tear out of the kiss, finding Lock there, sliding his fingers into my wetness. "Delicious, isn't she, brother?" Lock says, a prideful grin on his face.

"Without question," Talon says, drawing my face back to his and claiming my mouth.

The push-pull between them has the breath catching in my lungs and sets each of my nerve endings on fire. Talon backs away suddenly, dropping into the chair opposite us.

"Bend her over it again," he demands.

Lock spins me around, gently pressing on my spine until my breasts are over the chair, my arms hugging it for balance. My line of sight is directly on Talon as Lock steps up behind me, smoothing his hands over my spine before he nudges my legs apart. He drags his hard cock through my wetness, teasing me as he slides from clit to slit over and over again until I'm gripping the chair so hard my nails dig into it and Talon is grinning as he watches me squirm.

Lock plunges inside me then, and I gasp as the force of it pushes me harder into the chair. Talon's eyes are liquid fire as he watches, holding my gaze as his brother fucks me from behind. Over and over again, Lock thrusts in, holding fast to my hips and pounding into me so hard and fast where I can do nothing but hold on as he owns every inch of my pleasure.

And right when I know I'm going to orbit out of this universe, right when I'm going to shatter into a thousand pieces…

Lock slows his pace so suddenly I whimper.

"Lock," I whisper, my breath ragged.

"Yes, darling?" He leans over me, kissing between my shoulder blades and sending warm shivers all over my skin.

"Please," I beg, trying to move back against him, but he's holding me too tight, keeping me on the precipice.

Talon smirks and shifts in the chair, his cock already hard again as he watches the game.

"A little louder, darling."

"Please, Lock," I say loudly, speaking to him, but my eyes are on Talon, whose gaze is somehow like a caress over my skin.

Lock slams home again, and I moan. "Again," he demands.

"Please, Lock. I'm burning for you. I'm aching. Please—"

Lock unleashes himself on me, pistoning his hips as he slams into me from behind, reaching one hand around my hip to stroke my clit at the same time he hits that spot deep inside me—

My entire body convulses with the intensity of my orgasm, and I shatter entirely. I clench around his cock, pulsing through the throes of it as he finds his own release inside me. And he holds me there, planting kisses all over my back until we've caught our breath.

My eyes are heavy with exhaustion, but Talon's are wide and hazy. "You think we're done with you?" he asks right before he snaps his fingers and points to his lap. "Come sit."

Lock laughs darkly, then shifts out of me, freeing me to do as Talon says.

My legs are shaky as I pad over to Talon, who immediately grabs me and hauls one leg on either side of his hips. Settling my still dripping pussy right over his cock. "Talon," I gasp. "I'm still—"

"I don't fucking care," he growls. "You're mine." He slants his mouth over mine at the same time he shoves me down on his cock.

The sting is delicious and a hundred-percent Talon. His hands slide down my legs and leans me back slightly, grabbing my ankles and hooking my legs on either side of the arms of the chair, spreading me wide and stealing any leverage I may have had before.

He drives into me as he holds onto my knees, his eyes between my legs, watching where his cock slides in and out of me with abandon.

Something silky slides around my neck, a cool kiss of Lock's shadows wrapping around me and tipping my head all the way back. Lock is there, his black hair hanging down around his face as he leans over me and kisses me with an almost gentleness compared to Talon's fucking.

I moan into his mouth as Talon ups his pace, his hands gliding over my thighs and to the small of my back, hauling me against him, my legs spread so wide he slides in deeper with each thrust. Lock kisses me through my moans, drinking them in as that shadow keeps my head back, focused on him. He grazes his hand over my shoulder and down my chest, grabbing my breast and pinching my nipple until it's peaked, then does the same to the other one.

Lock loosens the shadow at my neck, and I look down, finding Talon watching Lock's hands on me with fire in his gaze. I reach up and brace my hands on his shoulders, my nails digging in as he relentlessly claims my body, giving me everything that is him and taking all that is me while Lock continues to tease my breasts and kiss my lips, my neck, my back.

Everything inside me narrows to the two sensations, to the slick caress of shadow and the stinging delight of pain, to the slickness between my thighs put there by both of them, and to the building storm climbing inside me.

I keep hold Talon's shoulder, then use my free hand to grip Lock's on my breast, clinging to them both as they have their way with me. And when Talon shifts, scooting us to the edge of that chair, leaning me back into Lock's waiting arms, his mouth claiming mine before I can even breathe, everything inside me coils like a hot spring ready to snap. Talon pushes in and out of me, his hard cock gliding over every hot edge I have, searing and sweet—

"Fuck!" I gasp into Lock's mouth as Talon drives into me deeper, harder, wrenching an orgasm from me that shakes my body and has me gripping them both like lifelines as I'm swung from one side of bliss to another.

"That *mouth*," Lock says against my lips, his tongue claiming my mouth with teasing flicks and consuming laps.

And then Talon brings his hand down on my clit in the lightest of slaps, jerking my entire body to attention, waking up my soul and sending me right into overdrive as he takes me harder, faster, until my next orgasm finally rips *his* from him and he spills inside me.

My body is limp as Lock holds me up, and Talon scoots me closer, the three of us breathless as we come down. I reach back and graze my hand over Lock's cheek, then do the same with my other hand to Talon.

"Take me to bed, mates," I say, my voice weak with what they've done to me.

Talon slides his arm around my lower back, holding me against him as he stands and walks us to my bed, Lock settling in on the other side as we climb into it.

And for a moment, sandwiched between two of the loves of my life, I'm able to hang suspended in the moment between us—the charged, electric current that ripples between each of us.

I'm able to pretend that leaving them here won't be the biggest regret of my life, or the most selfish.

I'm able to pretend that I'm only going to the kitchens for some hydration when I slip out of bed and leave the two of them sleeping so deeply they don't even stir when I slide into my fighting leathers.

And when I stand in the doorway, gazing back at my mates, knowing it may be the last time I see them, I'm able to pretend that I'm the villain in their story, the one I was always meant to be. I turn and shut the door, locking them inside.

They can't follow me. Not with my father waiting for me, knowing I'll come for Gessi. I have no doubt he's planned this all along—the attacks on the elemental realms, the dead All Plane soldiers, and now my best friend. He's proving his point, showing me I'm powerless against him, and he's using her as the light to guide me home.

He wants me to be the assassin he raised and the queen he arranged for me to become.

He wants me to bend and scrape and serve.

He should know better, but then again, I don't think my father has ever truly known me before.

But he's sure about to fucking find out just who exactly he's dealing with.

# 17

# CARI

*H*ome.

I've come home.

The midnight ocean churns behind me, the waves stretching along the black sand beach like it's reaching for me. Night blooming flowers scent the air, and a lump forms in my throat as I make my way toward the coves I know by heart.

I love my Isle, but the male who raised me here in lies and hate? He's turned my people against each other, him and his general have twisted our home into a warzone my people may not survive. And he's taken my best friend to use her against me in the midst of all the rest.

I may be home, but I'm not the same Shattered Isle princess I was when I left. I've grown into the female I've always been meant to be—partly because of my mates, but mostly because my eyes were opened to the truth, which had always been hidden from me. And now I want better for my people, for all the realms that have suffered at the hands of my father and his general.

They're dead.

They just don't know it yet.

I slip underneath the obsidian cove, the moon casting it in a silvery glow. The cavern smells like the sea and sand as I go deeper, gliding my hands over the craggy rocks until I find the hitch for the passageway Gessi and I made ages ago. Sparing a glance over my shoulder, I pause, something prickling over the back of my neck. I expected to see a guard or two by this point, but the beach is silent, the coves empty.

Luck?

I doubt it, but I don't have the luxury of waiting to find out.

I press against the hitch in the stone, the false wall giving way. I step underneath it, sealing it closed behind me as I'm thrown into darkness. My heart wrenches in my chest, knowing I've left my mates behind, but I push past the pain, assuring myself that their safety means more than their anger when they wake. I will not make them pay for the sins of my father, will not make them suffer because the stars chose them a mate sired by their enemy.

I will finish this and apologize later.

Walking by memory alone, I plunge deeper into my Isle, until I'm underneath the palace where the tunnel ends. I take a steadying breath and push against another false wall, stepping into the grim light of the dungeons. I keep my footsteps light as feathers and keep ice hovering in my palms as I scan hallway after hallway, cell after cell.

I keep to the shadows, the soothing darkness reminding me of Lock as it gives me cover when a few guards walk by. None of the prisoners hear or see me, but there are too many in these cells. The area reeks of filth and tears, the pleas of the prisoners offering more cover for sound than I could've hoped for. I leave them behind, hating that I can't spare them until I've found my father and the general and ended them— if they're innocent, like Gessi said the last time we spoke. No doubt there are fewer criminals in here, especially when the general delighted in converting thieves and killers into pets.

I climb the levels, clearing every area and growing more anxious with each cell I find that isn't holding Gessi.

Did the Shattered Isler who Steel and Blaize questioned lie to them? Did he plant this information so I would walk into a trap?

The sudden smell of orchids and the sea brings tears to my eyes as I round a corner in the upper level of the general's dungeons, and I quicken my pace, following my friend's signature scent until I come to a barred door.

Relief barrels down my spine at the sight of her, sitting in the corner in a chair, no doubt of her own making. She's gazing out a window, the night sky sparkling in between the bars.

"Gessi," I whisper.

She whips her head in my direction, shock widening her eyes as she leaps from her chair, sprinting to the door. Her auburn hair is caked with the dankness of her cell, but she's woven flowers throughout, and a broken laugh rips from my lips because only Gessi would grow flowers in prison and put them in her hair.

"I'm here," I say, and grip the bars of her door, frost coating every inch of them.

"Cari," she says, then darts her eyes behind me. "No."

I whirl around and jolt.

"Crane," I whisper-hiss, keeping one hand on the bars, freezing them to a brittle frailness, and create a dagger of ice in my other hand.

His green eyes look pale in the moonlight illuminating the hallway as he steps forward, arms resting at his sides.

"Don't," I warn, raising that ice dagger. "I don't intend to kill you tonight, but I will if I have to." A conflict rises in me, my history with Crane marring my judgment—I've known him as long as Gessi, as long as Varian.

"Aren't you going to tell her?" Crane asks, eyes on Gessi as he takes another step closer. "Aren't you going to tell her how I threw you in there? How I've stood guard every night? How I'm the monster she should most certainly kill?"

Gessi's breathing hitches behind me, and I glare up at him before glancing back at Gessi, who stumbles back from the bars, shaking her head, pain churning in her eyes.

"Is it true?" I ask.

"Cari, look out!" Gessi calls, and I whirl around. Crane rushes toward me, raising his boot.

I send my dagger soaring, but he knocks it away with a gloved hand, his damn hawk-like eyes seeing it before it can make its mark. I draw ice into my palms, preparing to encase his boot in a block of it, but his kick lands just past me—

And goes *through* the bars I've frozen, crumbling them to bits.

He steps back. "You don't have much time," he says, eyes on Gessi before he looks down at me. "Get her somewhere safe. *Please*, Cari."

Gessi's hands are over her mouth, shock rippling from her as I beckon her forward. She falls into my embrace and we cling to each other, tears rolling down our cheeks.

"I knew you'd get here," she says, releasing me.

"No one imprisons my handmaiden," I tease her. She knows she's so much more than that to me—a friend, a sister, a soulmate.

"Yes, because we have time for that," Crane whisper-snaps at us, and I turn on him.

"Where is my father? The general?"

"No." He shakes his head. "Get her out of here. Take her to whatever sky ship your mates have and keep her safe—"

"I'm done running," I cut him off. "And Gessi is perfectly capable of handling herself."

"She's proven that much," he snaps. "Being imprisoned and all."

"No thanks to you," she hisses back.

I clench my eyes shut. "He's right," I finally say, then flash Gessi an apologetic look when she gapes at me. "About not having time for this—"

"Right you are, daughter," my father's voice booms from the head of the hallway. "You are very, very much out of time."

Crane immediately grabs Gessi, wrapping his muscled arm around her throat. "Caught this one trying to escape, your highness," he says, and Gessi jerks against him, parting her lips to protest, but he clamps his hand over her mouth. "Should I move them both to a new cell?"

The general's boots shuffle against the stone as he walks up behind my father, his skin sallow, his thin lips pulling back to reveal those razor sharp teeth.

Fuck.

I'd hoped to find them separately. Facing them together?

I swallow hard, my heart breaking for my mates. If I die, they will never forgive me.

"That won't be necessary, Crane," I say, putting all the authority of the All Plane queen into my voice.

"And why is that, daughter?" my father asks, calm and collected, not at all bothered by my appearance in his dungeons.

Anger sizzles in my blood, and I raise my hands.

"Stop calling me that," I snap. "I stopped being your daughter the day you tried to kill me."

A slow, prideful grin shapes his lips. "What should I call you then?" he asks. "Traitor? Betrayer? All Plane whore?"

I clench my jaw, my body shaking from the adrenaline. "You can call me *queen.*"

His eyes flare, the only show of anger he lets slip.

"Crane," the general says. "Kill Gessi if Cari tries to do anything against her father's wishes."

"Yes, sir," Crane says, the voice of a Shattered Isle assassin— cold, emotionless.

I cut a glance at him, then to Gessi. That's the thing about sisters. We've spent enough time together to hold entire conversations without speaking. Gessi nods, her fingers curling around Crane's bicep at her throat. I have no idea where he stands, but neither of us is willing to risk it.

I shift to a defensive stance, sizing up both my father and the general.

This is going to hurt.

"And what is it you want from me, father?" I ask, taking a step closer, putting myself between him and Gessi.

"What I've always wanted," he says. "Power over the realms." He grins as I stop just in front of him, not a hint of a threat in his eyes as I stand so close. "And you're going to give it to me." He looks over my head, to where Crane still holds Gessi. "Or I kill the thing you love most."

Gessi isn't the only thing I love most. I have four mates who've claimed my heart and soul, but he won't get them either.

I shake my head. "You're operating under the assumption that Crane is a match for my friend," I say, then laugh. "He isn't."

My father's eyes widen at the same time I hear Crane groan, the snapping of tree branches crackling in the hallway as they wrap around his limbs and jerk him away from her. Gessi spears one of those branches just past me, so fast and hard I can feel the wind on my face as it hurtles for the general—

He catches the speared end of the branch in his hand, then snaps it over his knee, a grim smile on his face. "Foolish whores," he spits.

Ice flares from my palms, hitting my father square in the chest and propelling him backward and out of the hallway. I toss a glance over my shoulder, noting Crane grabbing Gessi again as she whirls on him, her fist cracking across his jaw. Something flashes in his eyes, but he doesn't strike back, and she continues to throw punches as he drags her down the hallway until they're out of sight.

I spin around, racing after my father, but an arm darts out, laying me out flat, my spine cracking against the hard stone floor.

"You want him?" the general asks. "You have to best me first."

I scramble to my feet, shooting a spear of ice at him, but he dodges with a swiftness that shoots me straight back to my youngling days, struggling to beat him every night to please my father.

I rush him, the rage in my blood propelling me forward, hands sharpened with ice claws as I reach for him—

He backhands me so hard I fly out of the hallway and into the wide-open room where we'd trained so many times before. My father has already taken his seat upon his throne on a dais across the room, settling in for the show.

Pain lashes through my body as I push to my feet, two ice daggers forming in my hands. I swipe at my nose with the back of my hand, my dark blue blood slicking my skin.

"Wouldn't it be easier," my father says from where he sits. "To simply give me what I want? You have the power to do it. You can grant me the ultimate position over the elemental realms and the Shattered Isle, then keep the All Plane for yourself."

The general steps toward me, malice flickering in his eyes as he purses his lips. An icy chill rakes down my spine as if I can sense the evil wafting off of him.

"I would leave you and your mates be," my father continues. "If you merely let me have what I want—"

"For what?" I snap, keeping my eye on the general as we circle each other. "So you can rule with fear and pain? So you can sic this monstrous creature on anyone who dares disagree with you? So you can delight while your own Isle falls into an internal war?"

"The fault isn't mine," my father says. "The people are fighting because those who are loyal to my reign do not take lightly to the rebels who are openly challenging me."

"And the ones who are starving? The ones who lost their sons and daughters to your war? What of them? Are they rebels? Who would love a king who does nothing but lie, manipulate, and take, take, take? I've never once seen you give anything to our people but nightmares, and I will not stand for you doing the same to other realms. You will not get what you want out of me, father. You never will."

A heavy sigh heaves from him. "Then Gessi is as good as dead," he says with cold calculation. "And your mates will be too," he continues. "After I've used you to force their hands in the same way you should've yielded with Gessi."

I'm not shocked by his threats or the icy way in which he casts me aside as a mere tool to be used to his advantage. There is no more room in my heart for shock or surprise.

Only revenge.

"You underestimate Gessi," I say, knowing she will hold her own. "And you've always underestimated me." I throw one of my daggers, too fast and sharp for the general to follow. It sinks into his right shoulder so hard he's thrown back a step.

He rips it out, blood spurting from the force, and roars as he charges me. I throw dagger after dagger, but he dodges them, and then an invisible force yanks me backward, pinning me to the ground as the general leaps atop me.

I pound against that force, trying to break it, but I've never broken it before. I turn my head to the side and glare at my father, who's wielding his power over me, just like he used to when I was young, when the general showed any signs of losing to me.

"You will bend, daughter," he says, then looks to his general. "Break her."

The general peels his lips back, exposing his needle-like teeth, and sinks them into my forearm.

I scream loud enough to rattle the stone walls.

# 18

# TALON

*I*t takes me all of two seconds to realize Cari is no longer in bed with me.

And all of one to leap out of that bed and race for the door—which she's locked.

"Lock!" I yell, and my brother groans awake.

"You're ruining a perfectly good dream," he says as he opens his eyes. It takes him even less time to catch up, and in seconds he's sliding into his clothes.

"She left." He doesn't pose it as a question, simply says it and glares at me.

"I didn't do this," I snap.

"No, of course not, brother," he says, rolling his eyes. "I told you all this would end badly, but does anyone ever listen to the chaotic brother? No."

"Now is not the time—"

"It really isn't," he cuts me off, then melts into shadows that slip beneath the door. A few seconds, and he jerks it open from the other side. He smirks, pride flickering in his eyes. "How much of a head start do you think our mate has?"

I don't share his sense of pride or anticipation as I tug on my clothes. Memories of last night tumble through my mind, the way I'd fucked her in that chair, the way I'd held her in my arms as she slept, the way I'd watched my brother bring her to the brink of madness time and time again. She'd done it on purpose, my villainous little mate. She'd made sure Lock and I were exhausted, and now? She could be suffering sun knows what.

My body shakes as I stomp through the ship, Lock on my heels as I make it to the cockpit—

"Sun save us," I groan, noting that we've already landed, and —according to the data—we'd landed an hour ago. "An hour," I answer Lock, and he shakes his head.

"She'd be back already if she'd bested her father," he says, and something hard punches the center of my chest.

Memories of the first time I set foot on this Isle blast through my mind, the vision of my mother and a sword run through her…

*Cari.*

"No," I breathe the word as panic climbs up my throat. "I will not lose her here. I will not!"

"We'll get her," Lock tries to soothe me. "She's strong—"

"So was our mother!" I snap, and Lock flinches.

I press the buttons on my hands, closing my eyes as my custom armor slides into place, the computer inside whirring to life. "Locate Cari," I demand and wait.

"You don't need a machine," Lock chides me. "You have me." He closes his eyes for the briefest of moments, then snaps them open. "She's in trouble," he says, and before I can ask, he shifts into shadows again, whirling around me so fast I can do nothing but follow where he leads.

He manifests himself outside the cove we picked to infiltrate, and doesn't hesitate to dash inside. I'm right behind him, my heart racing, my gut churning.

"Lock," I say when we've reached the tunnel's end. "If she's harmed...I won't be able to...I can't..."

"I know," he says, and there's a look of such murderous rage in his eyes that I suddenly pity those who have fallen in his path. A shiver of fear races over me, and in that instant, I realize that losing Cari will destroy *me*, but Lock could very well destroy the world—

A scream cracks the surrounding silence, and my lungs freeze as I lock eyes with my brother.

"Cari," we say in unison, right before Lock melts into shadow, disappearing so fast I can barely follow him, even flying.

# 19

## CARI

*T*he general's head wrenches back, his teeth ripping out of my arm so fast I yelp. A tree branch wraps around his neck, throwing him off of me and across the room.

I move to mend the wound with snow and ice, but I'm still pinned down by my father's power.

"I told you to stay behind!" Crane snaps at Gessi as he chases after the general.

Gessi is wielding her glorious earth powers, snapping branch after branch along the general, pounding him against the wall until he spits blood. But even then, the bastard breaks through, charging at her and Crane, who keeps himself between the general and Gessi.

Shattered Isle guards spill into the room in droves, rushing to their general's side.

"Traitor," my father says, eyes on Crane. "Kill him," he orders the guards.

Crane spins around, facing them even though he's outnumbered—

A dark beast leaps into the room, shaking the ground as he lands at Crane's side. Wide white eyes and glistening teeth stare down the guards coming for Crane, and they *hesitate* at the sight of Varian.

"Good of you to show," Crane snaps, reaching behind him for his signature bow and arrow. He nocks one and lets it fly, the arrow's tip finding home in a guard's eye.

"Couldn't let you have all the fun," Varian says, his voice rough and slightly garbled from his shift. He enlarges his obsidian arm and swings it out in front of him, taking down three of the rushing guards.

Gessi battles the general behind me, and I struggle against my father's power, desperate need to help her.

"You have poisoned too many people on this Isle, daughter." Father rises from his throne, stepping down the dais, his massive steps rumbling the ground as he slowly walks toward me.

He's going to kill me.

He's going to rip my head from my body as he holds me down.

He's going to…

*"Mate,"* Lock's voice slides into my mind. *"We're coming."*

"No," I say aloud, my heart racing in my chest. I don't want them anywhere near here.

I can't…I can't…

"No?" Father says as he nears me. "You aren't in a position to bargain."

I close my eyes, quelling the panic lashing through my body, threatening to choke my airways, threatening to numb me while my father rips me to pieces.

Memories flare in my mind of that day in the All Plane, the one where he nearly killed me, killed my mates.

Never. Again.

"No," I say again, focusing on my power, wielding it to latch onto my father's, to infiltrate it like Talon would a computer, like Lock would a mind, Steel a heart, or Tor the sky. I pull on the bonds thriving inside me, the power radiating between me and my mates, and I put everything I have into wrapping my power around my father's, unlocking it, cracking it, weakening it.

He doesn't seem to notice as he stops next to me, looking down at me like I'm a bug to be crushed. "You are the biggest disappointment I've ever endured," he says. "And remember, I've lost a *war*."

His words are meant to sting, to wound, but they bounce off my shield as strong as Steel.

"I should've ripped you out of your mother's belly and tried for a son. Instead, I let you kill the one creature I ever truly loved."

Tor's lightning deflects the barb as I meet my father's gaze.

"You will live only long enough for your mates to watch you die."

Lock's shadows sweep into my mind, calming me, focusing me.

"And only when they agree to my terms will I grant you that peace."

Talon's anger and punishment flare as bright as hot iron in my heart, but I don't dare move. I let my father see the wounded daughter, let him see the meek princess, let him bend down and get close enough to wrap his hand around my throat and squeeze.

My eyes widen around his grip.

"You will know nothing but suffering from here on—"

I shove a jagged blade of ice into his neck, a scream wrenching from my lips.

Father's eyes widen, shock radiating as he loses his grip on me and drops to his knees, the ground shaking as he paws at the blade in his throat.

But it's no use, I sunk it too deep.

I scramble to my feet, tears filling my eyes as I watch blood bubble from his lips.

"My..." he garbles. "Power..."

"Is smaller than mine," I snap, fingering the bruises I can already feel forming around my throat from his grip.

Not the first time, but it *will* be the last.

He coughs, choking on his own blood as I meet his eyes. "Tell me again how I'm going to suffer, Father. Tell me again how you're going to delight in my torture. Say you're going to harm Gessi or my mates *again*."

Father moves his lips, but only blood bubbles out. A flare of his power lashes out at me, but it's too weak to hold me. The life in his eyes flickers out, then he falls face first on the floor where he made me bleed so many times before.

"Didn't think so," I say.

Shadows gather across the room, and Lock immediately throws himself into the battle, fighting back the over-whelming number of guards near Varian and Crane. Gessi is in a heap, eyes closed—across the room, and there is no sign of the general.

I blink out of the shock of killing my father, my ears clearing and opening to the chaos around me. Screams and groans and cries of pain.

I take two steps, but Talon slams in front of me, his armor hard as iron as I bump into it. He removes his helmet, eyes panicked as he grips my shoulders. "Are you hurt?" he gasps, looking me over, noting the bruises on my neck, the blood on my face.

"I'm okay," I say, but he's shaking his head, his breathing erratic as he continues to look me over.

"Are you hurt, mate?" he asks again, frantic, his face trembling.

"Talon," I say, grabbing his hand and placing it on the center of my chest so he can feel my heartbeat. "I'm okay. I'm okay," I say again, and he blinks out of the panic, the emotion switching to anger.

"Don't you ever fucking do that to me again," he snaps before crushing his mouth against mine. "I can't lose you. I can't."

"I know," I say, tears in my eyes. "I'm sorry." I push past him, needing to get to Gessi, and slide to my knees when I reach her. "Gessi," I say, hauling her into my lap. "Wake up. Please wake up."

She's breathing, but doesn't stir when I gently shake her. I glance across the room, where Crane and Varian and Lock are rounding up the last of the guards who have surrendered, but more than a dozen lay dead on the floor.

"Lock!" I yell, and he snaps his gaze to mine seconds before his shadows bring him to my side. "Please," I beg. "Go into her mind. Tell me she's fine. Tell me she'll be okay…"

"Gess," Crane's voice echoes from behind Lock as he rushes over, Varian shifting to his normal self behind him.

"You fucking took your eyes off her?" Varian snaps at Crane.

Crane glares at him, the two facing each other in what will surely break out into a brawl.

"Not now!" I demand, the authority and panic in my voice ricocheting off the walls.

The two split up, going to either side to stand and watch.

Lock smooths his hands over Gessi's temples, his eyes closed. "She's there," he whispers to me. "She's there, darling."

"Who's there?" Gessi whispers as she opens her eyes.

"Thank the stars," I mutter, flashing Lock an appreciative glance as Gessi slowly rights herself.

"Did we win?" she asks, rubbing at the back of her head, her fingers coming back stained with her jade-colored blood.

I jolt at the sight. "We need to get you to the healer," I say, but her eyes are focused on something behind me.

"You did it," she says, looking at me. "You did it."

I glance behind me, noting my father's lifeless body, then scan the area for the general. "Not entirely," I say, then glance to Varian. "Find the general."

"I don't take orders from you, princess," he says, a smirk on his lips.

"She is your queen," Lock snaps, but Varian holds up his hands.

"I'll find the general, mind fucker," he says. "Don't get your shadows in a bunch." Varian shifts, the beast overtaking his skin before he sprints out of the room.

"The general escaped?" Gessi asks.

"We'll find him," I say. "But first, healer."

"I've got her," Crane says, reaching to scoop her off the floor, but Gessi glares at him.

"Don't touch me," she snaps, and the pain that radiates through Crane's face hurts even my heart.

"Lock..."

He doesn't need me to say more. He bends down, gently lifting Gessi into his arms before he glances at me. "Think about where the healer is, darling." I do as I'm told, and he nods. "Good girl," he says, then winks before his shadows swirl around them both, whisking them through the palace.

Crane races after them, leaving me and Talon alone with a half dozen bound and gagged guards.

Talon, no longer in his armor, is standing and looking down at my father's lifeless body. I hurry to his side.

"He killed my mother," he whispers.

"I know," I say, winding my fingers through his.

"And you killed him," he says.

"I did."

Talon turns to look at me, two tears rolling down his cheeks. "You left us behind," he says, and the betrayal in his tone hits me square in the chest.

"I'm sorry," I say. "I overheard your conversation with Steel. I couldn't bear the thought of Gessi being hurt—"

"We would've helped you get her out—"

"And you would've been in his path too," I say. I reach up and cup his cheeks, wiping away those two lone tears. "Do you think I'll gamble with your life any more than you'd gamble with mine?"

He grips my wrists. "But you gambled with yours, Cari. You could've been killed."

I nearly was, but he doesn't need to know that.

"I will spend every night and every day making it up to you," I assure him. "I couldn't risk you, Talon. You have to know that. Understand that—"

His mouth cuts off my words, melting us into an embrace that is angry and forgiving at the same time. And when he draws away, he pins me with that fiery gaze of his. "This isn't over until the general joins him," he says, pointing down at my father.

"Then let's go find him and finish this," I say, and Talon steps back, sliding his armor into place before scooping me up in his arms, and flying us out of the room.

# 20

# CARI

"It's been two weeks," I say, trying to keep the bite from my tone as I address those in the throne room. It gives me chills to be in this room, in the Shattered Isle palace that acted as my prison for most of my life, but it's the most logical place for a meeting like this. "The general did not simply vanish without a trace," I continue, shifting at the table where we all sit. It's a long, rectangular monstrosity that my father loved, but it's all we have for now.

"That's not entirely accurate," Crane says from the opposite end of the table where he sits near Varian, Steel and Blaize across from them. Lock is on my right, Talon on my left, Tor and River next to him, and Gessi next to Blaize. Tor, Steel, River and Blaize arrived as fast as they could after we sent word to them about my father's death.

"Do you have more to add to that, *bird boy*, or are you just making blanket statements?" Blaize asks, and the two glare at each other from across the table.

Gessi barely holds back a soft laugh, and I arch a brow at her. She shrugs, but my heart is at ease with the sight of her. She's fully healed and free, and that is what matters most to me.

"The general's powers were a well of secrets," Crane continues as if Blaize didn't just rib him. "Some were known," he says. "His thirst for blood, the relishing of torture and ability to strike fear into his subordinates, but others he kept close to the vest." He shrugs. "Any one of them could've been invisibility or cloaking."

"Fuck," I mutter, and Lock purses his lips at me. "That makes sense," I say. "Father always sent him on the most sensitive missions. If he could do that…" Stars, he could be anywhere. In this room…

"He's not here, darling," Lock assures me, tapping on his temple as he leans back in his chair, the picture of confidence. "I would know."

I blow out a breath. Thank the stars for that.

"We have to double our efforts," I say. "The Shattered Isle is still in distress and there are too many wrongs to count that need to be set right."

Everyone nods at that, and at least we're in agreement there. We'd already released the innocent prisoners and filled their cells with the general's most trusted guards. The rest of the general's supporters scattered across the Isle once news spread of what I'd done to my father. And now, I had one more thing to do…

"The Shattered Isle needs a queen who will nurture it back to life while also ruling justly. A queen who will breathe new life into her people and who will help it thrive as the Isle it's always meant to be."

"And you'll be that queen for us," Gessi says, dipping her head.

I shake mine. "I'm the queen of the All Plane," I say, and smile at each of my mates. "I can't be in two places at once."

Gessi furrows her brow. "Then who..." her eyes widen and she shakes her head. "No."

"Yes."

"*No,*" she fires back.

"Gessi," I say, eying her the way I've done a thousand times when I need her to do me a favor. Although, this is the biggest favor I've ever asked of her. "There is no one else I trust as much as you to rule this Isle."

She gapes at me.

"You've grown up alongside me, raised on this Isle as one of its own. You may have been born of the Earth Realm, but you were meant to rule in this one. Your kindness is unmatched as is your ability to see both sides of a situation and find the best outcome. You are perfect for this role."

"As *queen,*" she says, eyes wide. "That's not a job, Cari. Hand-maiden was a job. This is..."

"I know I'm asking much of you," I say. "And I'm sorry. I have no one else I can entrust my Isle too."

"We're sitting right here," Varian says, scoffing at me. "I'd have this place in tip-top shape in no time."

"Stars spare us," Gessi says, shaking her head. "Your choices are limited." She eyes Varian, who blows her a kiss. She quickly focuses on me.

"Even if I had a hundred choices," I say, reaching across the table to grip her hand. "I'd still pick you." I lower my voice. "You know this is right, Gessi. In your heart, you know you belong here."

She squeezes my hand, understanding and maybe a hint of panic flashing in her eyes. "I'll do my best to make you proud," she says.

"You always do," I say.

"What's my new role?" Varian asks, and I arch a brow at him for interrupting my moment with my friend. "What?" he shrugs. "We all know Gessi is queen material," he says. "She always has been."

I release her hand, settling back in my chair.

"Am I going on a hunt for the general?" Varian asks hopefully.

"No," I say, and he tilts his head. "With the general's whereabouts still unknown, and the need for me and my kings to get back to our realm to ease the tension there, Gessi's protection will be of the utmost importance."

Varian cocks a brow at me. "You want me to babysit, Gessi?"

A lush green vine snaps his chest from across the table. "I don't need babysitting," she says, and he flashes her a look that promises repayment for the vine slap.

"Of course you don't," I say. "Queens need protection. You, Varian, along with Crane, Blaize, and River, will be her new personal detail."

River dips his head, having already been brought up to speed on his new role earlier.

Blaize doesn't even blink, his eyes cast inward at some thoughts I won't even begin to try to analyze. Talon had argued against my choice of him, but with what Steel told me about him, and his help when we were under attack in the Fire Realm, I want the male guarding my friend. The general is a slippery monster, but he'd have a hard time breaking through the guards I've selected for her.

"You expect me to work alongside All Plane pretty-boys?" Varian wags a finger between Blaize and River.

"I can get you a picture," River says. "If you really think I'm pretty."

I bite back a laugh, as does Tor at River's side.

"Blaize?" I call down the table, and he blinks out of his internal thoughts.

"Yes?"

"Are you all right with your position or do you want to complain as Varian is? Now is the time." I certainly wouldn't be hashing this out beyond this meeting.

Blaize looks down the table at Gessi, almost as if he's sizing up her worth. "I will protect her with my life," he vows, and warmth spreads across my chest.

I glance to Talon, giving him a silent *told you so,* which he adamantly ignores.

"Thank you, Blaize." I look at Varian. Waiting.

"Fine," he says. "I'll play bodyguard for you, Gessi. Can't be much different from the games we used to play as younglings, right?" He smirks at her, and I glance between the two, curious.

Gessi narrows her gaze on him, then dismisses him completely.

*"Are you sure we can't stay a little longer, mate?"* Lock asks inside my mind. *"This looks positively entertaining."*

I bite back a smile, then subtly shake my head at him. *"We have a kingdom to get back to."* I remind him.

*"I do love seeing you in a crown,"* he says, winking at me.

Steel clears his throat. "That's really unfair," he says, eyes on me. "You two speaking like we're not even here."

"Steel," I say softly. "I'll fill you in later, I promise. I always do."

"You better," he says.

"I second that," Tor agrees.

I've missed them so much, and we've spent the better half of these two weeks making up for lost time, but somehow, it's not enough. Being separated from my mates is truly dangerous for everyone involved.

"Gessi," I say. "The Shattered Isle is yours, along with the palace. You can show River and Blaize to their new rooms, which I suggest are as close to yours as possible. I already have a team assembled to help you make changes." I glance to Varian and then Crane—who has remained silent since I named him one of Gessi's personal guards. "I would advise you two to move your things out of the assassin's quarters and near Gessi's."

"Of course," Crane says, dipping his head, but his green eyes are somewhere else entirely.

"I rather like my rooms," Varian says. "I'll stay where I'm at, but don't worry. It won't make my bodyguard skills any less effective."

I blow out a breath, then wave him off. Gessi will have her hands full with him, but she can hold her own. I'm sure she'll have them whipped into shape in no time.

"Then we're all settled—"

"Who's searching for the general?" Blaize asks.

"We've assembled a team of All Plane and Shattered Isle soldiers," Tor explains. "They will hunt him down, unless he's stupid enough to make a play on the new queen, in which case, that will fall into the hands of you four." He motions to River, Blaize, Varian and Crane.

I push back from the table. "Now that we're all settled, I need the room and Gessi."

The males file out, and no sooner have the doors shut than Gessi is standing before me, shaking her head at me. "I can't believe you did that!"

"What? You know you're meant to be queen—"

"Not that!" she cuts me off. "The guards! Crane? And two All Plane males I don't even know or trust?"

"You told me Crane saved you the night of the battle," I explain. "And River and Blaize are two of the best All Plane warriors I know, beyond my mates. They will keep you safe—"

"I can keep myself safe," she snaps.

"I know that," I fire back. "But, Gessi...I almost lost you. The general had you captive for nights on end, and any of them could've been your last with his taste for bloodshed." The words catch in my throat, a lump forming there. "I can't bear to think of that again." I shake my head.

Gessi wraps her arms around me, and we cling to each other.

"They're more for my peace of mind than yours," I say, holding her tight against me. "How am I supposed to go to the All Plane without ensuring you have every advantage at your disposal?"

Gessi laughs, releasing me. "Disposal is the optimal word," she says. "If Varian or Crane cross me, I will see to their hasty disposal."

We fall into laughter at that.

"Spoken like a true queen," I say, reeling it in. "And you'll love River," I continue. "I adore him."

"And Blaize?" she asks. "He's looks just as easily to kill me as to protect me."

"Yeah, he casts that vibe," I say. "But he's loyal to Steel, and Steel is the most honorable male I've ever met."

"That doesn't mean Blaize is," she counters.

"No," I say. "It doesn't. But it does point to his morals, which can't be altogether skewed if he cares for Steel as much as he does."

Gessi blows out a breath. "Queen of the Shattered Isle," she says, then looks at me. "And queen of the All Plane. How did we get here?"

"A lot of pain and bloodshed, as any ruler does," I say honestly. "And now is our chance to change things. To usher in an era of peace."

"It won't happen overnight," she says. "There will be those who disagree with both of us sitting on thrones and wearing crowns."

"Let them," I say. "Let them doubt us. We'll prove to each of them our worth by our actions. They've always spoken louder than any political promises ever could, anyway."

"You're not wrong," she says, and we walk arm in arm toward the doors. "What if the general comes for me?" she whispers.

Ice kisses my fingers. "Then you can delight in watching your personal band of assassins rip him to shreds."

A smile lights up her eyes as the image plays out in her mind. "Crane should be shirtless when he does that," she teases.

I nudge her, and our laughter echoes down the hallway as we walk headfirst into our new lives.

# 21

# CARI

*I* lean against the gilded balcony attached to my personal chambers in the All Plane palace, watching as the sun sets, transforming the sky from a burnt orange to a soothing lavender.

The royal city is preparing for their nightly rituals—shutting down shops and closing doors, settling in for a long sleep. Though, after yesterday's official release that the stars are no longer to be feared, there are still a few lights twinkling far below. It gives me hope, but I know change will take time.

It's been ten days since we arrived home, leaving the Shattered Isle and its people in the capable hands of my best friend, who I already terribly missed. Luckily, those on the Isle who knew me and knew Gessi were easy to accept her new role as queen when I made the public announcement before we left. But, just as for the All Plane, I know true change will take time. We've paid for the right to change things for the better with our blood, and with the general still on the loose, I fear more blood will be demanded before we see the end of terror across the realms.

"Have I ever told you how much I love seeing you wear that?" Steel's voice is a welcome comfort behind me, and I turn around, leaning my back against the balcony railing.

I glance down at the simple yet elegant gown I wear—a sleeveless number in the royal colors of the All Plane—gold and deepest red. "This?" I ask, smoothing my hands over the luxurious fabric.

Steel, clad in a royal blue shirt that clings to his muscles and black slacks, points to the top of my head as he walks over to me.

"Oh," I say, laughing slightly as I finger the crown atop my head. My long hair hangs in waves over my bare shoulders beneath the crown, which is decorated with gold and rubies, gilded in a way to make it look like the sun itself is kissing my brow. "I think I'm getting used to wearing it."

Pride and love beam from Steel's eyes as he leans over the balcony railing next to me, his sky-blue eyes looking down at his city far below. He wears his own crown of gold and rubies, sitting in a simple band atop his head.

We're so high in the palace we could very well touch the clouds, but I much prefer to watch the stars awaken each night, marveling at their glittering glory as they stretch out over a midnight sky.

"It suits you," he says. There is a contentment shaping his features that has been present the last few days, and it fills my heart. There is still much to heal from, both losses and histories to grapple with, but each of my mates has found a sort of inner peace these past days since we've settled back in the All Plane.

"Have I told you how much I missed you?" Steel asks, turning his eyes away from his city and planting them on me instead.

I bite back a smile. "Several times," I say, butterflies flapping in my stomach. I don't think the sensation will ever go away, the overwhelming amount of love I hold for each of my mates, the way they can each surprise me, excite me, challenge me. "Have I told you how much I missed you?" I tease. He knows. I've made it abundantly clear to him and Tor that I never wish to be separated from them for that long again.

Though, I'm not naïve. I know the responsibilities of our roles as kings and queen will send us to opposite ends of the universe at times, but for now, I'm content to surround myself with them as much as possible.

Steel grins at me, hooking one of his impossibly powerful arms around my hip and sliding me before him, caging my back against that railing as he brings our bodies flush.

Heat races up my spine, little shocks bursting everywhere our bodies touch. He smooths a hand over my cheek, looking down at me with a smile on his lips. "Never again," he says, before brushing his lips over mine in the softest of kisses.

"Never again," I repeat against his lips, even though we both know very well we can't control the future.

Steel moves his lips to the corner of my mouth, then down the line of my jaw, and down my neck, leaving a trail of internal fire everywhere his lips touch. The pressure is soft yet somehow searing as he makes his way over my breasts, teasing me over the fabric of my gown.

Content. That's the only way to describe the slow, sensual way he's exploring my body, as if we truly have all the time in the world.

And, for now, I suppose we do. Or at least until one of his brothers comes to demand my attention. My toes curl in my high heels just thinking about it.

I shift, cupping Steel's face, as he's made his way back up to my lips. "How did I get so lucky to have you as a mate?" I ask, emotion clogging my throat.

Steel's eyes gutter, his power flaring down the bond with strength and pride and love.

"We're the lucky ones, my queen," he says, and this time when our mouths meet, there is a sense of urgency to the kiss. A hungry tangle of tongues and nips that send my heart rate soaring.

Steel breaks out of the kiss, pulling me away from the balcony railing just enough to spin me around to face the sky. He brushes my hair to the side, his fingers eliciting warm chills as he slowly unbuttons my gown. It falls in a puddle of silk at my feet, and he kisses his way down my spine, hooking his fingers into the hem of my lace undergarments and pulling them down my legs until I have to step out of those too.

The night breeze is crisp against my bare skin, and Steel turns me around to face him again, his eyes trailing over my peaked nipples, and lower to between my thighs, my heels still on. I reach for the crown atop my head, prepared to slip it off, but Steel grabs my wrists with uncanny speed.

"Leave the crown on," he demands, and a warm shiver rushes down the center of me.

"You too," I say as he pulls his shirt over his head, then loses his pants, his cock springing free in a way that makes my eyes widen. I'll never get used to it, the passion between me and my mates, the need to consume each other, and I never want to.

Steel reaches for me, pressing me against that balcony as our mouths meet, his tongue sweeping between my lips, thrusting in a way that is merely a preview for what is to come. His hands slide down my bare arms, over my curves, until he grips my hips and hauls me up, perching me on that balcony in the sky.

I gasp, clinging to his shoulders.

He grins at me. "Do you trust me?"

"With my life," I say.

"Good." He lowers himself until he's eye level between my thighs, one strong arm hooked around my lower back to keep me right where he wants me. "Look up," he says, a smirk on his lips, his breath warm against where I'm aching for him.

I arch my head back, and at the same moment my eyes land on the freshly bloomed night sky, Steel licks straight through the heat of me.

"*Steel*," I moan, my nails digging into his shoulders as he licks and laps, his warm mouth and slick tongue turning me wholly liquid for him. He plunges his tongue inside me, fucking me like I know he will with his cock.

The stars glitter above us, the entire sky stretching out above us, encompassing everything in a sparkling darkness that suspends time.

Steel holds me steady with one arm, his other hand trailing up my leg and between my thighs, two fingers replacing his tongue. He pumps me while planting teasing kisses on my clit, giving me the lightest of pressure when I want more, *need* more.

"Look at me," he demands, the vibrations of his words ricocheting deep inside me. I glance down, finding his blue eyes churning, a prideful grin on his lips. "I want to see your beautiful face when you come in my mouth."

A hot shiver makes my body tremble, and he slides his fingers out of me, replacing them with his tongue before he flattens it against my clit, rocking it up and down, over and over again until everything inside me bursts in a million pieces of starlight.

His name is a plea on my lips as I hold his gaze, my thighs clenching around his cheeks, and he laps me through the throes of it. And only when my breathing has evened does he plant one last kiss on my oversensitive flesh and pull away, rising to meet me at eye level.

"The sky has nothing on you," he says, and my heart expands in my chest.

I cup his face, drawing his mouth to mine, kissing him soft and languid, the way he's made my body feel, before I shimmy off the railing and slide down his body, dropping to my knees before him.

Without hesitation, I take him in my mouth, sucking him in to the hilt so fast he jerks. I moan around the taste of him, slicking him with my tongue while I bob up and down, eyes flitting up to where he stands above me in nothing but his crown.

Stars save me, he's glorious. The power radiating down our bond fuels the hunger inside me. I can feel the tension in him as I tease and suck, can feel what he needs from me—

He shifts away enough that his cock springs from my mouth with a little pop, and I arch a brow as I look up at him.

"When I come," he says, gently gripping my chin. "It's going to be inside you."

I smile up at him as he hauls me to my feet. "Take what you need from me, my king," I say, and he shudders against me.

"Are you sure?"

I love him all the more because he always asks, always makes certain that I want him unleashed, unchained, and unhindered.

"Always," I say, smoothing my hand up his cheek before tangling my fingers in his hair. "I'm your *mate* and you are *mine* and you will not hold yourself back. Not here. Not with me."

Steel leans down, pressing his forehead against mine. "I fucking love you," he growls before hauling me off my feet, his sheer strength managing the move in one graceful motion.

One second I'm standing before him, the next my thighs are clutching his hips and he's pressed my spine against the palace wall on the balcony, his cock situated right where his mouth made me slick for him.

He supports me with one muscled arm beneath my ass and plunges inside me with one powerful thrust. His eyes are on me, searching for any hint of pain from his strength.

"*Steel.*" His name is a demand from my lips, and I crush my mouth against his, hard and fast, showing him just how fine I really am.

He groans, his free hand slamming into the palace wall, cracking the stone as he thrusts into me again and again, his power building and swirling around that bond between us as he lets himself go completely.

"You. Feel. So. Good," I say, each word cut off by a moan as he slides in and out of me, his hard length filling me so much I can barely think or feel around the sensation. He reaches the spot deep inside me, hitting it with a pressure that builds and builds.

He moves me effortlessly, using that hold on my ass to heft me up and sink me down on his cock as he thrusts, turning me into a puppet at his mercy. And stars damn me, I can do nothing but cling to him while he wrenches pleasure from me that I can feel along my bones.

My fingers splay against his muscled chest, and I kiss him between breaths as he has his way with me. Over and over again, he fills me, pumps into me, drags himself out of me only to start over again.

My mate. He's heat and life and hopeful promises while he fucks me with the night sky glittering behind him, our bond flaring and sparking with each of his strokes.

I rip my mouth from his, my entire body trembling as another orgasm builds and twists inside me, winding me up so tight I know I'll snap any second. I catch his gaze, watching those blue eyes churn as he fully lets go, pistoning his hips into me so hard and fast I turn into a breathless, wild thing as he shoves me over that sweet, sharp edge.

I clench around him, my orgasm slicking me even more as I flutter around his cock.

"Cari," he groans, his fist slamming into that wall again, the cracks deepening as he comes inside me with a growl.

His thrusts slow, working us both down as he kisses me breathless.

"I love you," he sighs between my lips.

"I love you," I say right back, my body going limp in his arms as he tugs us away from the wall. I glance back at the damage he did, noting the cracks spreading out from a Steel-fist-sized epicenter.

"I'll get someone to fix that," he says, an almost shameful look in his eyes.

I grip his chin, forcing him to look at me. "Don't you dare," I say, then glance back at it. "It's beautiful."

"But—"

"I'm your queen, am I not?" I tease, and he cocks a brow at me.

"Yes, you are."

"Then do as I say, husband." I grin down at him, flicking my tongue over his lips.

He shudders against me as he walks us into my chambers, heading straight for my bed. He lays me down, smoothing his large hand over my stomach and up over my breasts. "Yes, my queen," he says, and I swear I nearly come again from those words alone.

* * *

"The statistics are in," Storm says from his spot at the opposite end of the breakfast table. "Our new All Plane queen is becoming more popular among our people."

Anticipation flares in my chest. "Are you being truthful?" I ask. With Storm, it's hard to tell, but Talon nods from where he sits next to his friend.

"He is," Talon says.

Lock slides his hand along my thigh underneath the table. "Of course, they love you, darling," he says.

"Not, of course," I say, but I'm smiling all the same. "I'm still the daughter of an enemy. I know it will take time—"

"You slaying your father might have something to do with their liking you," Tor cuts me off, popping a strawberry into his mouth and winking at me.

That wink sends me spiraling into a well of memories from this morning when I'd awoken chained to the bed by bands of delightfully shocking but pleasurable lightning.

"Any word with how our friend River is faring with his new charge?" Storm asks, leaning back in his seat.

"I spoke with Gessi yesterday," I say, flashing Talon an appreciative look. CB-1 hugs my neck, his gentle whirring a constant comfort and connection to my best friend. "Things are…progressing slowly," I admit. Gessi may have said if River tinkered with one more object of hers in an attempt to improve it, she may send him back to me as a piece of furniture, but they didn't need to know that.

Storm laughs, shaking his head as he rises from the table. "I miss that bastard," he says, then bows to me and my mates.

"I'm off on my official royal duties," he says, then glances at Talon. "I've assembled a secondary team, like you requested. We'll be on the hunt alongside team one until we finish this."

A cold chill races down my spine, and Lock shifts his hand higher, as if he can sense the fear in me.

"We'll find him," Steel says from my other side.

"Do I get some kind of reward if I do, your highness?" Storm teases.

"What would you like?" Talon asks. "You already have everything you could ever want."

Something flashes over Storm's features, but it's gone in a blink, replaced by the over-confident smile I've become accustomed to from him. "There is always room for more," he says, then bows again before zipping out of the room so fast he's gone before I can draw my next breath.

"Do you ever get used to that?" I ask.

"No," each of my mates says in unison, and my heart fills as we fall into laughter.

We're here. Each of us. Ruling the realms together in a way that is just and right and ensures growth. I honestly couldn't ask for anything more.

Well, except for maybe the general's head on a platter.

"What's on the schedule today?" I ask.

Steel shifts beside me. "We have a public appearance in the afternoon to deliver much needed provisions to the less fortunate part of the royal city."

I nod. "And before that?"

"Wide open, my queen," Steel says, and I grin at him.

"In that case," Lock says, sliding out of his chair so swiftly it doesn't even make a sound. He tugs on my hand, taking me with him. "I'll be keeping our mate occupied until the public appearance."

I gape at him, heat rushing over every inch of my body.

"That's entirely unfair," Talon says, but there's a lightness in his eyes that screams nothing but happiness. "Then I get this evening."

Steel sighs. "Tomorrow morning is mine."

Tor's lightning crackles through the room. "You'll have to beat me there," he says to Steel. "You didn't this morning."

All my mates turn to look at me, as if I somehow had anything to do with the scheduling of their time. I laugh, grinning at them.

"I'm yours," I say to all of them.

"And on that note," Lock says, smirking at his brothers before shadows swirl around us, suspending us in a sea of silky darkness that lifts my feet off the ground. I have the sensation of flying, but I have no idea where Lock is taking us, and I certainly don't care.

Our kingdom is healing.

My best friend is the queen of the Shattered Isle.

My mates are happy.

And the forever stretching out before us is the kind dreams are made of.

"Where shall I make love to you today, darling?" Lock whispers in my ear, and I can barely sustain my grin at what has quickly become our special little game.

"Anywhere," I say, sliding my hands up his chest, looking up into his blue-green eyes as the shadows continue to swirl around us. "As long as I'm with you."

## THE END

Thank you so much for reading! If you enjoyed Gessi's character and want to find out what happens when River, Blaize, Varian, and Crane become her personal assassins be sure to check out the sneak peek of chapter one of her story, THE ASSASSINS below! Coming Summer 2022!

# THE ASSASSINS SNEAK PEEK

**Gessi**

"*I* can't believe you agreed to this," Blaize snaps from behind me.

"She's our queen," River chides. "What would you have me do? Tell her no?"

"I would've," Varian chimes in, the hint of utter annoyance in his tone.

As usual, Crane is silent as the night where he brings up the rear of our little group.

I roll my eyes and whirl around on the rocks in which we're trekking over. "I am standing right exactly here," I say, looking at each of them and having a hard time disguising the intake of breath the sight inflicts upon me.

Truly, this group of males is one to marvel at. Each one is uniquely different and yet somehow just as annoyingly attractive. Varian and Crane I've known since younglings, but they've both grown into formidable males with skills and powers and muscles for nights on end.

But the two All Plane warriors? Stars damn me, I never thought it possible to be attracted to beings so inherently different. River is all sunshine and jokes and laughter with a body that's carved like a block of cedar, and Blaize? I don't even know how to describe him with his bedroom eyes, inky hair, and glittering silver tattoo along one arm that begs to be touched, the lines of artwork and stars traced.

Luckily for me, they're all insufferable and incessantly annoying with how seriously they take their duties as my personal guards—*thanks so very much, Cari.*

"Yes," Varian says, stepping up onto a craggy rock and towering over me. "We can see you, your highness. Just as well as we can see how ridiculous you look out here, braving the southern villages in some fool heartedly attempt to lure out the general yourself." His tone is sharp, his eyes narrowed and this side of agitated.

"You should watch your tone with our queen," River says, arching a brow at Varian.

Varian points at him. "And I'd watch yours, pretty one," he says. "Lest I watch it for you."

River blows Varian a kiss, which only makes a growl rumble in his chest.

I blow out a breath, dismissing the two, and shifts off the rock, heading for another one. They tried to stop me, tried to talk me out of venturing this far from the royal city, but it was no use.

"There have been attacks on this end of the Isle, attacks that scream of the general's penchant for torture," I say as I climb upon another rock, the sole of my flat shoes slipping slightly. "And I will *not* sit on my throne and wait for the monster to tear through what is left of my people. Like I said before, you all are with me or you're not." I spin around to face them, to show them how serious I am about not caring one way or another if they accompany me or not, but I lose my footing and fall backward, my spine no doubt aimed for the nearest, sharpest rock—

Strong, warm arms cradle me against an even harder chest. The scent of smoke and cedar swirl around me, sending a deep shiver right down the center of me as my eyes meet Blaize's. They're so light blue they're almost silver.

I swallow hard, my fingers digging into his leathers where he holds me against his chest—

"Clearly," Varian says, snapping me to attention. "You don't need our assistance, your highness."

Blaize blinks a few times before gently setting me on my feet and continuing ahead, clearly unaffected by me nearly plummeting to my death.

I blow out a breath. Maybe they're right. Maybe I'm in over my head. But am I really supposed to let that stop me from trying to spare my people any more hardship?

"If it's any consolation, my queen," River says as he walks by my side. "You fell utterly gracefully. Definitely no flailing of the arms or scrunched face." He presses his lips together, holding back a laugh that elicits one of my own.

I chuckle, shaking my head as we continue down the path. River, despite his antics with tinkering, always makes me laugh even when I don't want to. And I never knew how much I needed to laugh before he came into my life.

River winks, and my heart flutters as he walks ahead of me. It's an effort to *not* look at the three males ahead of me, their leathers clinging to every muscle and shift in their movements, but somehow, I manage it and forge ahead.

"Are you ever going to forgive me, Gess?" Crane's voice is a whisper at my back as he follows behind me.

I swallow around the lump in my throat, my heart clenching at all the things left unspoken between us these last weeks. He's tried on several occasions to explain his role in helping the general imprison me, but I've never let him. Yes, he helped me escape, but only after Cari showed up. No, I can't hear his excuses, can't bear to hear how the mission was more important than me, than the friendship I'd thought we held.

I hold my head up high, searching for a response as we climb another bank of rocks along the path, the difficult terrain the only way to reach the southern villages on the Isle. The rocks are slick from the wind blowing the ocean all over them, and stars damn me, I slip again.

Crane's fingers are warm on my elbow as he steadies me, and lightning streaks through my veins at the innocent touch. I pause, my gaze locking on his. He shifts closer, his dark spice and rose scent spinning my senses.

"Maybe I should carry you, my queen," he whispers, something molten in his eyes as he trails them over the length of my body. "You seem to be having trouble staying on your feet today."

I swallow hard, heart racing. We're too close, the others too far ahead of us. My body wars with my heart, which he thoroughly broke when he tossed me in the cell at the general's command, when he stood guard at my door every single night and watched as I was tortured until I couldn't scream anymore.

Tears fill my eyes and I jerk out of his touch. "I'd rather fall and break my neck than let you touch me again," I snap, and Crane flinches.

I hurry ahead, reaching the others as we clear the last of the rocks, the mountainous terrain yawning open to the sandy beach hugging the obsidian ocean, and the village scattered about it.

"We're here," Varian says, but his voice is low, rough, and a muscle in his jaw ticks.

I follow his gaze and gasp at the sight of smoke curling from what is left of the village—huts and buildings burned and destroyed, ash floating on the breeze like fallen feathers from overhead birds.

I push past Varian and River, stumbling toward the wreckage, my heart cracking down the middle—

"Don't," Blaize says, his hand on my arm as he hauls me back.

"I have to help them," I say, tugging out of his embrace.

He hauls me back, wrapping his arms around me from behind, my spine flush against his chest as he whisks us behind the nearest rock, shielding us from the sight of the ruined village. He spins me around to face him, his strong hands on my shoulders, and his eyes locking on mine.

"Those fires are still burning," he whispers, his voice one hundred percent All Plane warrior. "Whoever did this is close. You can't be spotted."

"I can handle myself—"

"I know that," he snaps. "But you're the queen of the Shattered Isle. Your safety goes beyond your capabilities. What do you think happens to your Isle if you're taken prisoner or fall under an enemy blade?"

My chest rises and falls, panic climbing up my spine at his words. He's right. Stars *damn* him, he's right.

"Do you have her?" Varian asks, no annoyance or cocky banter in his tone.

Blaize nods.

"We'll sweep it," he says, and motions to River and Crane, who follow him out of sight.

"Have me?" I glare up at him.

"I'll stop you," he says, shrugging. "If you try to run."

"I'm your queen—"

"And Steel asked me to protect you," he cuts me off. "That means I protect you, even from yourself." He presses closer, caging me between the rock and his body.

I tremble against him, some forbidden craving flaring to life inside me. Blaize is my personal guard and a near stranger. I have no business feeling…anything for him.

"Steel," I say, tilting my head. "Not your *king*?"

A slow, crooked smile shapes Blaize's lips. It's one of the first I've seen from him, and it makes my knees shake. "I'll never call Steel my king, and he knows it. An order from a king I can ignore," he says, and my brows raise at that. "But a favor for Steel?" he shakes his head. "I've never let him down before, and I don't intend to start now." He leans closer, eyes raking over every inch of my face. The breath in my lungs catches. "So, your highness," he says, and the title feels like a caress. "Are you going to make me stop you?"

My lips part. He's so close I can't breathe around his scent, can't feel the sea kissing my cheeks because his warm body is blocking it all. There is nothing but his consuming presence, his power crackling between us—

"My queen," River calls from around the rock, and Blaize puts distance between us enough for me to breathe, enough for me to blink out of whatever haze he'd put me under. "It's clear," he says when he's rounded the rock, and extends his hand toward me. "But there is something you should see."

I spare one last glance at Blaize, unable to read the emotion in his light-blue eyes, before I take River's hand.

He keeps hold of mine as he guides me down the beach and amongst the wreckage, until he stops before one home left completely intact.

I squeeze his hand in mine, drawing on his warmth and comfort to keep my knees from buckling. "Stars save us."

# LET'S CHAT!

I love hearing from you! You can find me at the following places!

Facebook

Facebook Author Page

Jadempresley@gmail.com

And be sure to sign up for my newsletter here for release information, cover reveals, and giveaways!

# ACKNOWLEDGMENTS

A GIANT thank you must be paid to all the amazing, badass booktokers out there that have been so amazing and supportive! The list below is just a snapshot of the wonderful readers out there and if I missed your name, PLEASE know that I see you and appreciate every mention, video, comment, and message! I love you all!

@tiffandbooks @winterarrow @trishaarwood @pixiepages @oliveroseandco @thebookishgirlreviews @asthebookends @breanna_reads @booksdanirreads @songreads @erynsarchive @yelenabooks @hdouglas92 @leggothemeggoreads @klaudias_bookdiary @libraryofmadison @stakestheworld @thebookcloud @spicybooks @sami_cantstopreading @rachies_book_nook @dealingdreams @booklovingcorgimom @coffeeandbookswithlauran @lokiquinn1993 @nightowlbooks @bookofcons @animebaby33 @muddy_orbs @crysreads @biblio_mama @briannareadds @morallygrayreads @fortheloveofbooksandwine @natashareadsnrambles @pagel_bagel_ @nerdy_julith @bookishmot

Another huge thanks to Amber Hodge for editing this and making it sparkle! I couldn't do this series without you!

A bit thanks to my husband and family who always indulge me when I get lost in the writing cave.

Thank you to all the amazing readers for picking this up and taking a chance on four delightfully different brothers! And finally, a huge shout out to all the Marvel fans who just want a little more sometimes :)

# ABOUT THE AUTHOR

Jade Presley is a pen name for a fantasy and contemporary romance author who loves cranking out stories about seriously sexy males and the sassy women who bring them to their knees. She's a wife, mother, and board game connoisseur.

Made in United States
North Haven, CT
09 August 2022

22446811R10153